AN CARLITO'S WAY

Rise to Power

Edwin Torres

Black Cat
New York
a paperback original imprint of Grove/Atlantic, Inc.

Originally published in 1975 by Saturday Review Press/
E. P. Dutton, New York

Printed in the United States of America
Published simultaneously in Canada

FIRST EDITION

Library of Congress Cataloging-in-Publication Data

Torres, Edwin.
Carlito's way: rise to power / Edwin Torres.
p. cm.
ISBN 0-8021-7012-9
1. Hispanic American criminals—Fiction. 2. Organized crime—
Fiction. 3. New York (N.Y.)—Fiction. I. Title.
PS3570.O697C37 2005
813'.54—dc22 2005045984

Black Cat
a paperback original imprint of Grove/Atlantic, Inc.
841 Broadway
New York, NY 10003

05 06 07 08 09 10 9 8 7 6 5 4 3 2 1

*To the memory of Orlando Cardona,
the best of the 107th Street bunch, killed in action,
February 4, 1951, Wonju, Korea*

Introduction

Americans made more Western and gangster flicks than any other genre. And in a way the gangster flick is the urban Western. The city replaces the wild, wild West, where anything is possible—the American dream, for any bad motherfucker tough enough to grab it; the immigrant fantasy of infinite possibility, but not without a price; complete with gamblers, con men, fast women, and of course, the outlaw or the gangster. *Carlito's Way* has all that. As a filmmaker I've done both Westerns and gangster flicks, but what hit me when I first read Eddie Torres's book was the voice: rich, authentic, and lyrical like the sway of a Latina's hips, with the mystery and undeniable rhythm of the street, like congas pounding beneath her strut. From page 1 you smell the fried onions, the bodegas, the cheap perfume of young whores, and the stench of back-alley wino piss.

This is not a lofty prince's tale of heroic deeds. This is the gritty story of an urban cowboy's rise to power. A member of the *lumpenproletariat,* someone uncomfortably close to us, or rather the us we fear we could be if dealt similar circumstances. There but for the grace of God go we? This is the tale of a flawed Everyman, trying to get loot, get laid, and survive with a modicum of dignity in a world bent on kicking his New-Yorican ass.

In an age where some heads of state view the world in terms of an axis of evil and "evildoers," then by logical extension there must be "good doers." This reductive perspective leads to a polarized good guy vs. bad guy look at humanity. The reality, of course, is that we all have the capacity for good and evil, and that complex grey area in between is the stage where writer Eddie Torres dances.

His Honor Torres, a practicing New York City judge, writes of outlaws without ever casting the stone of judgment at his subjects. As Bob Dylan sang, he "knows too much to argue or to judge." Torres takes us on a tour through the fertile underworld of the fifties and sixties where good guys and bad guys were often one and the same. Using rich Latino ghetto prose we follow our lead character, Carlito Brigante, on an odyssey through post–World War II New York City during a time when American apartheid was alive and well.

Carlito, a product of Spanish Harlem, seems wonderfully ignorant of the turbulent political times surrounding him. A survivor, a Po-rican caught between the Italians on one side and the blacks on the other. He is a minority of minorities, unwilling to bow or to bend in a world where the rules are laid down by the "haves" to keep the "have nots" from ever having. Overtly apolitical, Carlito seems instinctually aware of the injustice inherent in the system, and the "isms" that inevitably go with it: lookism, sexism, racism, classism. He is a man conscious of his own mortality and limitations and the cost of standing up in a world designed to keep the underclass down. The nail that sticks out is the one that gets hammered upon.

Frantz Fanon points out that the most successful colonizers always left behind the church and the schools, to socialize the oppressed to the oppressor's point of view. (If Brother Frantz was alive today, he'd probably add films to that list.)

Interesting that Carlito seems suspicious of both; like a con man sensing some greater systemic con, he avoids any doctrine, academic or religious, that would have him kneel and pray for pie in the sky.

He lives by his own moral code, the code of the street, the "hodedors," at a time when there was still honor among thieves. Carlito is a gentleman rogue, a product of the juvenile detention centers, raised without a father, and having lost his mother at an early age. Carlito learns to hustle, having decided early on that he'd rather be a hammer than a nail, a fucker than a fuckee.

While doing a stretch in the joint he is adopted by his only true family, his big brothers and future partners in crime—Rocco Fabrizi and the character I play, Earl Bassey.

Meanwhile on the outside, the civil rights movement is starting to gain momentum. During the sixties Dr. King is calling for freedom by "peaceful means" from the pulpit of the black Baptist church. Uptown in Harlem at the Muslim temple Minister Malcolm X is calling for freedom "by any means necessary." At the end of his arc, Malcolm returns from his pilgrimage to

Mecca and talks of having prayed next to Muslims of all colors. He goes international, reframing the issue of civil rights as one of human rights. Malcolm moves to bring these issues into the World Court of the UN and broaden his constituency. He becomes a perceived threat to the status quo and is taken out. When King reaches across the cultural and racial divide, marching on Washington with people of all colors, taking a stance on American poverty and the Vietnam War, he too becomes a perceived threat to J. Edgar Hoover and the COINTELPRO gang and is soon taken out.

Staying in one's own racial or cultural box makes one vulnerable to the old divide and conquer, us vs. them, "evil doers" vs. "good doers" routine, but crossing the racial divide, connecting the dots, has always been a risky endeavor; doing so in the underworld of the sixties was no exception. These three brothers of other colors from other mothers—black, white, and Puerto Rican—get out of the joint and come together in spite of the odds. It is interesting that the racial combination of young Carlito's two surrogate parents or big brothers, Italian and black, would yield something close to Puerto Rican.

These three men form an alliance, a brotherhood, ex- ploiting the racially divided underworld in pursuit of yet another color—green, the color of money—and in that sense their union is revolutionary. Carlito, Rocco, and Earl make their future in the illegal heroin trade, in the tradition of prominent Americans like Joe Kennedy, who profited from illegal alcohol during Prohibition. With an "if I don't deal it somebody else will" mentality, they are businessmen meeting the demands for their escapist product with supply. They are what the Black Panthers referred to as social parasites.

As Earl's pseudo revolutionary younger brother, Reggie, says in the film, "When the revolution comes the people are gonna line all of the dealers up with the other oppressors and gun 'em down."

With the death of both Malcolm and Martin, the colored community that once sang "We Shall Overcome" was righteously pissed off and started singing "Say it loud, I'm black and I'm proud." Across America there were riots. Voter registration by blacks shot up. Militancy was on the rise, young folks both black and white where organizing and protesting the war in Vietnam.

Some would argue that this rise in militancy was deliberately medicated with the influx of drugs into the inner cities. Junkies don't vote, organize, or question authority. Today's gangs inherited the bravado of the Black Power movement without the political ideology to support it. Any last songs of political protest or black pride were drowned out by the booming bass of the new so-called gangsta rap, extolling the virtues of mindless capitalism and taking it to new levels. Why just put the gold around your wrist or your neck like the old-school gangsters when you can put the shit on your teeth too? Ghettos became "self-cleaning ovens" with gangs preying upon each other, adopting a genocidal, black-on-black, bling-bling, "I gotta get mine and kill my brother" mentality. Ultimately the FBI's COINTELPRO was a success neutralizing black leadership.The revolution would not be televised, it would implode.

In Elaine Brown's book *Taste of Power,* she writes that in the early seventies coke was starting to flood the ghetto and some cops were looking the other way. "Cocaine in Oakland is cheap now, no longer the drug of choice for the rich and famous, it's coming into Oakland at low prices from I don't know where. . . . Big-time dealers are establishing turf." Whether this was deliberate or not, no one could argue that although there were no poppy fields in the ghetto, and no gun-manufacturing plants, there was now an abundance of both drugs and guns in the hood.

The logistics required in importing this contraband across America's inner cities requires the cooperation of those significantly up the food chain from the Carlitos of the world. Torres's book ends before the superstar gangsters of the late seventies and eighties inherited the mantle.

Gangsters like Nicky Barnes, who was one of the models for Neno Brown in my film *New Jack City,* and who would grace the cover of *The New York Times* and earn the nickname Mr. Untouchable. Barnes did for narcotics what Ford did for the automotive industry. The new upstart dealers would not inherit Carlito's code of ethics. Mobsters would start to turn states' evidence, ratting each other out. The Carlitos, Roccos, and Earls of the world would be a dying breed.

Torres's book, an edgy social commentary on America's underworld, captures an era with an authenticity that makes one wonder if the good judge led a double life. Multiracial, visual, and brutally honest, it's no surprise that this book, like his others, has inspired a film: *Carlito's Way: The Rise to Power.*

—Mario Van Peebles
June 21, 2005

CARLITO'S
WAY

*S*OONER OR LATER, A THUG WILL TELL HIS TALE. WE ALL WANT *to go on record. So let's hear it for all the hoods. The Jews out of Brownsville. The Blacks on Lenox Avenue. The Italians from Mulberry Street. Like that. Meanwhile, the Puerto Ricans been gettin' jammed since the forties and ain't nobody said nothin'. We been laid, relayed, and waylaid and nobody wants to hear about it. Well, I'm gonna lay it on you one time, for the record.*

Who these people? Puerto Ricans. They come from an island a hundred long by thirty-five miles wide. They come in all sizes, colors, and shapes. They got a little of everybody. Heart like the Jews, soul like the Blacks, balls like the Italians. They hit New York in the 1940s, the wrong time. But like when is it right, when your face don't help, your accent ain't French, and your clothes don't fit? They hung in anyway—most of the tickets were one way. So they filed into the roach stables in Harlem and the South Bronx. They sat behind the sewing machines

1

and stood behind the steam tables. In other words, they busted their ass, they went for the Dream. Most of them.

A handful couldn't handle the weight at the bottom of the totem pole. They wouldn't squat, couldn't bend. Had to take their shot. Them was the hodedores, *hoodlums. Hard nose. And like the thugs from any group they went for the coin of the realm, head on.*

I'm talking from the far shore looking back on thirty years. At least I made it to the other side. Most of my crew got washed on the way. And if survivors don't talk about it, who's gonna know we was here, right? So here's how it went down for one P.R., me, Carlito Brigante.

1

I CAME ON THE SCENE IN THE 1930S. ME AND MY MOMS. Brigante Sr. had long since split back to Puerto Rico. Seem like we was in every furnished room in Spanish Harlem. Kind of hazy some of it now, but I can remember her draggin' me by the hand from place to place—the clinic on 106th Street, the home relief on 105th Street, the Pentecostal church on 107th Street. That was home base, the church. Kids used to call me a "hallelujah"—break my chops. My mom was in there every night bangin' on a tambourine with the rest of them. Sometimes they'd get a special *reverendo* who'd really turn them on. That's when the believers, *feligreses,* would start hoppin' and jumpin'—then they'd be faintin' on the floor and they'd wrap them in white sheets. I remember I didn't go for this part. I was close to my mom, it was just me and her.

I was comin' into my teens in the 1940s when they laid her out at Gonzalez's Funeral Home on 109th Street.

Looked like she was into one of her faints, like she'd
be all right. Wasn't like that. I ain't sayin' my way
would have been any different if she'd been around.
That's all you hear in the Joint—aw, man, I didn't have
a chance. Bullshit. I was already a mean lil' fucker while
my mom was alive, but I always respected women because of her.

Anyway, the court put me on to this jive uncle who
come out of nowhere up in the Bronx. I got promoted
from the basement to the sub-basement. No good. I cut
out. Back down to Harlem. Sleepin' on the roof. Stayin'
with friends. Then the juvenile people put me in the
Heckscher home near 104th Street. But I was always
takin' off on them. I was still in my teens. World War II
was over but they was warrin' in the streets. Kiddie gangs
was goin' strong. The Puerto Ricans was boxed in. Irish
on the south, Italians to the east, Blacks to the north and
west. Wasn't none of that brotherhood jive in them days.
Git that Po'Rican! We was catchin' hell.

The crazy part is me comin' up rumblin' against these
groups as a kid—it should end up that the only two cats
that was ever in my corner was Earl Bassey, a black dude,
and Rocco Fabrizi, a wal-yo. Unbelievable. But I'm
jumpin' ahead.

Lemme tell you about them rumbles. The wops said
no spics could go east of Park Avenue. But there was only
one swimming pool and that was the Jefferson on 112th
Street off the East River. Like, man, you had to wade
through Park, Lexington, Third, Second, First, Pleasant.
Wall-to-wall guineas. The older guys be standing around

in front of the stoops and stores, evil-eyeing us, everybody in his undershirt; the kids would be up on the roof with the garbage cans and in the basements with the bats and bicycle chains. Mostly busted heads, black eyes in those days. First into the street was always me, loved a swingout. That's when I first saw Rocco Fabrizi. He was running with a wop gang, the Redwings. One day we went down to the pool with about twenty or thirty P.R. guys—a hell of a rumble—and right up front is this guy, Rocco, swinging a stickball bat. Stuck in my mind, tough kid. We took a beating—their turf, too many guys. A while later we get the word that this Rocco is sneaking up on a roof with a Latin chick named Carmen—fine head—near Madison Avenue and 107th Street. The balls. He caught some beatin', but he stood up; the Lopez brothers wanted to throw him off the roof but I said enough. He remembered.

The spooks said no Ricans could go west of Fifth Avenue. So if they caught you in Central Park, shame on you. The Copiens, the Socialistics, the Bachelors, the Comanches—all bad motherfuckers—these were the gangs that started using hardware. Then the rumbles got mean—like if the Copiens caught you, you knew they were going to stick you. Then the zip guns came out, metal tubes with door latches as firing pins set off by rubber bands—if the pin hit the .22 on the primer and the piece was held close to your head, you were in trouble. Lucky for a lot of diddy boppers it wasn't often. I once got caught by the Copiens in Central Park by the lake near 106th Street. Me and this black kid duked it out after he said, "Let me hold a quarter." I said, "Let yo' mammy hold it." We got it on, I was kicking him on the ground when his boys arrived on bikes—my blood was up; I said, "I'll take any one of you motherfuckers." "No, motherfucker, we gonna kill yo' ass," and they started pulling the rubber bands on the zip guns. So like I quit the scene, they chased me all the way to 110th Street. That was the last chase on me like that. I always carried a piece from then on. I wasn't about to take no shit. You step up, I'm gonna knock you down.

Summers were hotter in them days. No air conditioning—the asphalt could burn your sneakers. Took the bus up to Highbridge Pool in Washington Heights. The Irish jumped us in the locker room—we fought with the metal baskets. Know what the pool guard said? "You don't belong up here." No sooner we was on the bus back, we had to bail out the windows on to Amsterdam Avenue, a mob of micks was comin' through the door after us.

That same summer I got hit in the head with a roller skate by some spade in Central Park by the boats near 110th Street. Another time I got my neck all scraped up from a bicycle chain some eye-talian wrapped around me. We caught it from everybody. Don't get me wrong, we gave good as we got—but you remember your own lumps better. We was tryin' to melt into the pot but they wouldn't even let us in the swimming pool. *Hijos de puta.*

Irregardless, I was never a race man. Us P.R.'s are like that—maybe 'cause we come in so many shades. We always had a stray wop or Jew-boy and plenty of spades with our gangs. Anyway, I figure them beatings get you ready for later on—when you gotta get the money.

But the clubs wasn't always fightin'. There was a lot of stickball playing—we had the Devils, the CBCs, the Home Reliefers (dig it), the Turbens (that's the way they spelled it), the Viceroys, the Zeniths, the Falcons, the Tropical Gents, the Royal Knights, the Boca Chica— these all claimed to be S.A.C.—social and ataletic club—ha.

Pimping was popular. Tony Navarro, the Cruz brothers, Bobby Roldan, all had whores. We looked up to these guys—big cars, always a ringside table at the Palladium: always clean, none of that zoot-suit shit—wingtip shoes, conservative-cut clothes. Imagine lookin' up to a pimp! Later on we wouldn't let one of them scumbag motherfuckers stand near us at the bar.

About that time *motherfucker* came into style—it came down from black Harlem in a game called "the dozens." Two cats would meet on the street and start playin' the dozens; one guy would say, "Ashes to ashes, dust to dust, your mother has a pussy like a Greyhound bus," and the other guy come back with, "The dozens ain't my game but the way I fuck your mother is a goddamn shame!" Rough on the mothers. From then on everything was motherfucker.

Mostly we stood around corners on Madison Avenue. Just like Middletown, U.S.A.—ha. The schools, Patrick Henry, Cooper—forget about it. No YMCA, no Boys' Club, no gym, raunchy houses, scummy streets. If you inclined to plea-cop, them streets contributed to the delinquency of a whole lot of minors. But who wants to hear that shit? Only plea I ever copped cost me three years in the slams. A man got to stand up. Take his shot.

Like when the junk started arrivin' about this time. And where did the wops first arrive it? Right on ol' 107th Street between Lexington and Third. A punk-ass kid I was, but I looked it over. I'm gonna ride the horse, or the horse gonna ride me? That was the question on a lot of them corners, 'cause the junk was still a new scene in the forties. All the losers went for the spike and the dynamite high behind it. Only a skag high ain't but good the first few times out, then you hooked, all they gotta do is reel you in, by the crotch now, and squeeze till you cough up another five dollars for a bag. I seen the horse play with them junkies like a cat with a rubber mouse.

Age fourteen, I saw that. I said, uh-uh. Them's the humped—I'm goin' with the humpers. The dealers had the pussy, the clothes, and the cars. That's what I wanted, in that order. The dope fiends had the sores, the scabs, the O.D.'s. Maybe that's what they wanted. Must be crazy—couldn't see it then, can't see it now.

I was thinkin' myself, among other things, half a pug in them days. I didn't really know the science of the game, but I was heavy-handed, with a lot of snap in my shoulder, so when I tagged a stud, he was hurtin'. So now I'm gonna go in the Gloves, this must have been round '48 or '49. With a little trainin' everybody said Carlito was a natural. I was gonna fight for the Police Athletic League. Ha. And who was the man there? Moran of the

Twenty-third Precinct, my sworn enemy. "What, this fuckin' troublemaker on my squad?" So I ended up fightin' unattached. My trainin' was drinkin' wine and smokin' pot. One time I ran around the 106th Street lake in the park—finished up puffin' on a joint. Some program for a contender. Irregardless, I kicked some ass down in Sunnyside and Ridgewood, including a bad spook from the Salem-Crescent A.C. But then they busted my jaw in a street fight on 105th Street and I had to drop out of the tournament. What a laugh on Moran if I had gone all the way to Chicago. Him with his squad breakin' their ass runnin' around the reservoir every day.

Anyway, I'm too good-lookin' to be a pug. I'm gonna be a pimp. I'm runnin' round with these fly broads from 111th Street and Fifth Avenue. That's where all the whores were trickin' in them days. Whores galores. But I could take a knock-around broad but so long. I didn't go for that scene too tough. Pimp got to hate women. That sure wasn't me.

There was some nice chicks around but their mothers wouldn't let them out the house. Specially with *delincuentes* like me waitin' on the stoop. Them was not "free sex" days. Leave it to me to come up at the wrong time. The good girls held on to their cherry. And it was a big deal. If a broad dropped her drawers, right away she lost her rating—even to the scrounge who copped them; "I ain't gonna marry no broad what lost her cherry!"

I used to get laid in Central Park, but you had to have a long switchblade ready 'cause always some degenerate motherfucker would be sneakin' up on you and your girl from behind the bushes. I didn't mind a guy lee-gating (peeping), I used to do it myself, but these pre-verts would want to gang-bang your broad. I chased more than one around that park at night. One guy tried to hit me with a wooden Keep Off The Grass sign, which he pulled out the ground while he was running from my sticker. He missed, I didn't. Many a piece I missed out on, gettin' interrupted by this element.

I was a big pussy-hound. Ain't changed much either.

Was a big movie fan too. Knock-around kids was always in the movie house. No TV in them days. The Fox Star on 107th Street and Lexington Avenue was our show. There was some bad guinea racketeers in there. You had to go with a gang, 'cause if the wops caught you alone on the balcony, you was a flyin' Po'Rican. I remember once they had a singin' contest on the stage on a Saturday. They was givin' ten dollars to the winner. I was there with a whole mob of guys smokin' pot in the balcony. I ran up on stage and sang "Bei Mir Bist Du Schön," which I sang as "My Dear Mr. Shane." I couldn't sing worth a damn, but you rated on applause and my people made the most racket. I won. Then I did "Playmate" and the dirty version of "La Cucaracha," which was my best number—they couldn't get me off the stage.

I was into being a musician too. This was 'cause I noticed they was gettin' all the fine women. Some ugly clown be shakin' maracas or a cowbell in front of a band and all the chippies be saying, oh, he's showbiz! Jive-ass bitches. Showbiz is the guy giving enemas to the elephants in the circus. Anyway, I got me a big conga drum out of the pawnshop and thought I was Chano Pozo, the great Cuban conga player used to work the skins for Dizzy Gillespie. Chano was the greatest. Bad too, big stud, used to be strongarm for the politicals in Havana. Came to Harlem, was bad there too. Somebody forgot how bad and blew him away. But he had some tough hands while he was around. My hands couldn't keep no beat, I was not about to be no great *conguero*. So be it. I'll get me that trim some other way.

Used to play at block parties—everybody in Harlem be there, dancin', drinkin', smokin', 'n fightin'. Had one on 107th Street, Copiens or Dragons came around— forget who—anyway, they started shooting pistols. My friend, Tato—"Carlito, they got me"—fell on his back under the lamppost. *Coño*, Tato, he's dead! No way, cap hit him on his belt buckle—didn't have a scratch. Just like in the movies. After that, I used to throw myself on the ground—"Tato, they got me!" I was a big ballbreaker as a kid.

But don't get me wrong, I used to do a lotta good things too. Although later on they never showed up in any of my probation reports. Like God forbid somebody abuse a buddy of mine. I'd travel for blocks to duke with a cat that would try to gorilla a friend—I tangle-assed with Sabu from 104th Street and Flash from 110th Street, bad motherfuckers in the first degree, and it wasn't even my beef. "This ain't witchoo, Carlito"—"Never mind, take to the street." That's the kind of guy I was. But some-times could backfire on you. Like m'man Políto—went up to 113th Street to straighten a kid out for somebody. Políto told me he was a stringbean black kid. Skinny arms and legs. Políto was a regular lil' buzz saw. He said shee-it, I'll tear 'im up. Políto say that spook kid like to bust him everyway but loose. Later on he found out the kid was Sandy Saddler.

One time I had to rumble a deaf-mute guy. On me like white-on-rice. Couldn't get off on this guy. Whipped me. I had respect for the handicapped after that.

A lot of Hollywood names in Harlem at the time. We had Tarzans and Sabus and Cheyennes. I remember a guy used to call himself Naiyoka—like from Pago Pago. We had Cochise and we had Apache. Sometimes a name could cause a problem. Like Cheyenne from the Bronx would come down with ten or twelve guys to see Cheyenne from Harlem—"Who said your name was Cheyenne?"—"Not me, my name is Jacinto Quinones." I seen that one. Then you had a pimp name of Red Conk on account of he conked his hair red (hair was straight in them days one way or the other—Dixie Peach or Sulfur 8). We had a white guy named Negro, and we had a black guy named Indio. We had a lot of Louies—Louie the Jew (crazy Jew got killed in a stickup, spoke better Spanish than me), Louie Lump-Lump (had a funny-shaped head), Louie Push-Push (used to run fast). We had Tobacco, Chuleta, Machete, Frankie *La Cagona* (Frankie the Shitter).

How'd I exist on the street? Somtimes legit—like delivery boy on an ice truck, or a grocery, or a dry cleaner's. But mostly hustlin', thievin', break and entry—shootin' pool was my main stick. I used to catch merchant marines for a hundred, hundred-fifty dollars playin' nineball—this when I was fourteen or fifteen years old—always had good wrists. Then there was boostin' in department stores—and there was dice, cards, writin' numbers (single action) for Jakie Cooperman, one of the few Jew bookies left around. We had a little scare with Jakie once. Jakie used to book out of a candy store on 108th Street and Fifth Avenue—he was a degenerate gambler himself. Me and some other kids were hangin' around one night. This big black car pulled up with four rays of sunshine—older wops from the East 107th Street mob out of the Fox Star. Two stayed in the car, two came into the candy store. Skinny guy, Nino, he had half a button, cool head, he'd talk to you. The other guy, Buck, was a terror—looked like a buffalo, only bigger—and he used to carry a softball bat—was the bouncer at the Fox Star. God forbid he should catch you sneakin' in the side door. Buck stands by the door, Nino walks up to the counter and pulls an empty bag out of his coat (the two of them was wearin' black coats and black hats with the brim turned up—wops got this Al Capone shit down to a science). Anyway, the bag was a cement bag. Nino gives the bag to Moe, owner of the store—"This is for Jakie." Moe shit a milk shake right there. Then Nino turned to me and the rest of the kids—"Anybody here seen Jakie around?" No, not us, never happen. They split. We was shook up. Seems Jakie was into the shylocks for fifty thou. The wops said he ran away to the coast on them, but Jakie himself would have given you five hundred to one he was planted on Long Island. Wops was already leery about goin' up to Black Harlem. Not Buck (really Buccia)—he'd jump out of a car on 116th Street and Lenox Avenue bat in hand—"C'mere"—spook would run—one shot—lay 'im out. Buck didn't give a fuck. He went up in the mob later on. Stayed mean.

There was other guys like Buck around. *Abusadores,* we called them—abusers or ballbreakers. Uptown Harlem had one named Jenks, or Jinx. Bad nigger. Big—didn't fit through no door, 'cept sideways. Take everybody off. Take your money, your welfare check, your watch, your dope—take a wheelchair, glass eye. Mean. When he was outa jail, people stayed home. Jinx had a pretty long run, then he tried to run a game on a friend of mine. Shakedown. So much per week 'cause I'm bad. My buddy was hardnose, so he had to deal with Jinx. Shot him in the legs—kept coming. Shot him in the chest—kept coming. Finally stopped Jinx with a bullet through his head. All this time Jinx was chasing him around the bar. My friend had to do time for this. Judge said, "Victim was unarmed"—that motherfucker was armed when he was unarmed. Some judges will say, "Why didn't you go to the police?" The fuckin' police only want to know you as one of two "de's"—de deceased or de defendant. In between—"Don't bother me, I got lotta paper work." If the judge took time to check out a "victim" like Jinx he'd give the defendant the Distinguished Bronze Cross, first degree. And if His Honor had to live in the same tenement with a Jinx or a Buck, he'd put the contract out hisself. Buck and Jinx—some neighbors we had.

Another source of livelihood for me was a first-class Murphy game I used to run up on 111th Street with the tricks looking for whores. Me and m'partner Colorado used pencil and paper (that would impress the Johns)— "Okay, write it down, eh, Chico? These two gentlemen, ten dollars a piece—that's twenty dollars. No rough stuff or fancy fuckin', boys; Lolita is only sixteen and just startin' out. I'll hold the money." Colorado would go upstairs, then he'd call down, "Lolita wants to see the money and the list first, Pancho." Wait right here, boys, she's very shy—I'll call you from upstairs. You could come back an hour later and they'd still be waiting with their hard-on. Lo-leeta, Lo-leeta, they'd be yodelin' in the canyon. Sometimes me and Colorado would fall down on the roof from laughing.

Them roofs was busy for us. Flyin' pigeons, flyin' kites, flyin' dope. Somebody was always jumpin' off the roof too. Usually some Rican who couldn't cut it on the street. But the street got him anyway—unless he jumped in the backyard.

Anyway, I was a busy lil' snot in them days.

SOMETIMES MORAN THE COP WOULD GET A BUG UP HIS ASS and grab me or Colorado on the street and put us back in the Home. Maybe a kick in the ass and a few smacks in the face from a telephone book in the Twenty-third

Precinct before he took us over. He wanted me to go over to another precinct to break chops—I said I was a citizen of this precinct and he couldn't deport me. To this day I don't pick up a phone that I don't say, "Moran of the Twenty-third Precinct." I used to do it then figuring the phones in the poolroom or the bar was tapped and Moran's name would get on some shoo-fly tape. He was a tough sombitch. One night, one of them traveling carnivals came to the lot on 108th Street and Madison Avenue. This guy Lucky ran out of luck in a fight with some marine tiger who cut him to pieces with a butcher knife. I remember him on his back on the ground trying to kick up at the guy. He never made it to the emergency table at the Flower Hospital. Moran was there with some photographers from *Life* magazine and he got a write-up with pictures and all. Lucky was a sharp dresser, used to be in the furnished rooms on 107th Street between Park and Madison. He didn't come out too good in the pictures though. Moran, believing his own publicity, became a worse ballbuster than ever.

Another ballbuster cop was Schula or Schuler, known as "Cara de Palo" (Woodface). He was a fat guy with glasses, but he could move, specially the time they threw the garbage can off the roof at him.

Baddest of the bad was Big Jeff from the "Mutt and Jeff" detective team from the Twenty-third. One was a little wop, Lil' Jeff, the other a big mick, Big Jeff; you couldn't call either one Mutt or they'd break yo' ass. When they'd pull up to the poolroom on 106th Street and Madison, everybody start walkin'. Nearly everybody.

Legend says that one time they wanted everybody lined up against the wall in the poolroom—"All you Puerto Ricans up against the wall"—this smart guy wouldn't get up—"Me no Puerto Rican, me Cuban"—*wap!* "Same shit." None of that "move-along-boys" jive in them days.

Little Jeff give you sass, Big Jeff look around like he ain't even listening, but if you gave backlip—wap!—Big Jeff laid you out. I ain't seen nobody, in the ring or out, hit harder than him. Elbow close to body, leverage—lights out. Better you fell off a roof than he should land on you. Big Jeff finally got put out of commission by a little P.R. name of Augie Robles. Robles was a contract killer, one of the few we had around there. I mean this dude would travel to other states on hits. Around Harlem, he'd feed off the policy bankers. Like, "You know me, Augie Robles; you got a thousand for me by Saturday, okay?" Everybody was scared shit of him. Big Jeff and Augie finally got around to it on 112th Street. There must have been ten thousand people watching that shoot-out. Just like in *Scarface*. Big Jeff, as usual, was the first bull through the door. Imagine, Augie Robles, cornered, with four, count 'em, four pistols, waiting on you. Shee-it. The bulls killed Augie that night, but not before Big Jeff got his knee blown up with a dum-dum. They tried to do this gunfight in a jive movie, *Madigan*. Big Jeff make Madigan look like a faggot. He was bad. But he wasn't no flake artist. He let me walk away from one that wasn't my doing even though he could have laid it on me. Bulls ain't never been my bag—but here's to you, anyway, Big Jeff. You done the right thing.

The Ricans had some other hairy guys. Was a guy, Cabezon, sat down in a barber chair at Lino's on 107th Street off Madison—"Lino, cut my hair short today. Tonight I'm going to settle with a guy. No telling where I'm gonna go afterward." That's cold. He goed it too. Electric chair.

Then was a guy, Johnny Lata, had his face cut by a rival pimp, Tony Navarro. Lata kept a straight razor in a pan filled with onions and water so that when he got his revenge the scar on Tony's face would never heal. Lata did cut a forget-me-not on Tony's face, but the onion bit never checked out because Tony's liver gave out from too much coke not long after. Tony had in his stable of four the best lookin' whore in Harlem, a German war bride. When that *fenomeno* used to walk down the street I used to lay right down on the pavement—"Vee gates, fraulein"—but I was too broke to hit on her. When I think of all them fine women I didn't get nothin' of! Years later, after Tony died, I went to a party at Birdland and there she was with a spook band leader, one of the biggest in the country. Being broke never was no fun. I'll be dead or in jail, but I ain't ever gonna be broke. Believe that.

That's all I was ever interested in, makin' a dollar without hurtin' nobody. By my lights, I wasn't nasty or no troublemaker like them other motherfuckers around there; them guys was just burnin' up inside—the streets was battery acid to them. But the streets never whipped me that bad. I always saw the signs leading out—they was always painted green. Right this way, Mr. Brigante.

That guy Lino, the barber, used to worry about me. He was from the same mountain town in P.R. as my moms. They gonna kill you on the street, Carlito, they gonna lay you out in Gonzalez's Funeral before you're twenty-one. He wanted me to go to school like this guy on the block Wilfredo—imagine a grown man still going to school. Never learn nothin' out of no book. Keep your eyes and ears open, maybe read the *Daily News* to know who's gettin' locked up. If the smarts are there, you be all right—if they ain't, you can read books from shit to Shinnecock, ain't gonna help. Lino was a okay guy, used to bring me Baby Ruths when I was in the Home. He beat me to Gonzalez's. Here's to you, Lino—you done the best you could.

IN THE MATTERS OF RACE, THE PUERTO RICANS WAS AHEAD of their time in the forties. We accepted everybody. Nobody accepted us. Since black was not in style in them days, us P.R.'s declared ourselves white. We had a few variations but that didn't bother us none. The Cubans say, *El que no la tiene del Congo, la tiene del Carabalí.* Myself, I don't go for colored guys—but what about colored gals? This country can't do without them fine women— no kinda way. This country can make all them cars, toasters, ice boxes—goin' to the moon—meanwhile, it's still hung up on the race watzis. Bunch o' bullshit. If the rest of the country had listened to us it wouldn't be in the mess it is now. You take me for instance. I been light enough to sit in the front of a Jim Crow bus but dark enough to be worried about it. I been taken for spook, wop, and one faggot (used to come to the door jay-naked when I was delivering clothes for a cleaner) said I was Armenian. You're better off having a little bit of everything. That way you are what you have to be whenever you got to be. But who gives a shit, the main thing is to be good-lookin' so the broads will go for you.

Ricardo Montalban I ain't. But many a kitty has gone for me even when I didn't have big bread behind me. Believe that. It is true I spend all my time pursuin' good trim and, thank God, have a good rap. It is also true I have had knocked-out-lookin' broads. *Tremendos pollos.* White, black, tan, green, 'n in b'tween (never had no Chinese broad). In other words, I have done all right with the fair sex. I got no squawks in that apartment.

Fact is, I got no beef about my first twenty years. Had me a hell of a time. Warts and all, the streets was my playground. Couldn't ground me down—not the bulls, not the thugs, not the landlord, not the welfare, not no-body. I ran all over them. Fact is when I was in the get-o I didn't even know I was there. I didn't even know how dee-prived I was or that I was one of the downtrotted—it was news to me when the socio workers told me about it. I was happy as a pig in shit.

I would say by and large and mainly Carlos Brigante, mainly known as Carlito, had a good time as a kid. The next twenty years is more tricky. In other words, in the 1950s I was mostly a criminal. I have to admit that. And I did a lot of time for it too. But then Earl Bassey wised

me up and Rocco Fabrizi gave me a break into the heavy
wood. So like the sixties was big time for me and I was
less into bein' a thug and more like a class guy. But I'm
runnin' ahead again.

OKAY, THE END OF THE FORTIES SAW ME INTO THE SLAMS
at Elmira Reception Center, Elmira, New York. Thereafter known as "the El." First whiff of country air. Alma
mater for many a mope majorin' in thievery, roguery,
lechery, and mopery. Thirty-six-month bit I did. I had
been on probation for sticking a guy who'd busted my
jaw with brass knuckles made out of ashcan handles.
Probation don't mean I didn't have a few things going—
burglaries, cars, like that. So like I'm shooting dice on
105th Street off Madison Avenue on a Saturday afternoon when this bad-ass named Chago grabs all the money
on the ground and says, "These dice are loaded. You guys
are robbing me; I'm taking the money," and he pulls out
the difference, size .38, so I say, "Motherfucker, you ain't
going nowhere with my bread."

"I'll kill you, Carlito."

"Kill me, *hijo de puta,* kill me—"

Everything is real quiet now except for Chago's
breathing—he ain't got no heart. I grab the piece, bust
him in the face with it; he falls down some basement
steps, and I grab a garbage can full of ashes and throw it
on him. That night I'm shooting nineball in Ramon's
parlor on 106th Street and Madison when Mutt and Jeff
from the two-three squad come in.

"Chago's over at the Flower Hospital. He's asking for you, Carlito."

"Chago who? What right you—"

Smack. Right off my ear.

"Okay, let's go see him."

No lineup, no reading of rights—they even gave me an admission. Times were rough. Judge put me away— felonious assault, violation of probation. For Chago, they shoulda give me a medal.

In the Joint, thirty-six months. Up there I meet a lot of the boys, including Rocco Fabrizi, who was up for stealing cars. He was tight with Earl Bassey. Earl was up there for dealing in pot. I'd been hearing about him on the Street in Harlem, he was the war counselor of some click uptown on Lenox Avenue. Earl was around our age but he was slick beyond his years. He could see something coming around the corner, like he'd say, "So-and-so is a faggot," and there would be this big stud with tattoos and muscles blowing everybody in the Joint. He knew things. I can't explain it; he never went to school but he could read people in minutes. His skin was black, but his eyes were like yellow, and when he put them on you everything was cool, like calm. Nothing went down without discussing it with Earl. Even the hacks would check out a beef with Earl.

Me and him got real tight when I started boxing again. Even in the street when I was smoking pot and drinking wine, my hands were quick and my wind wouldn't quit. Like I'd get inside a cat and hook to the body—I'd catch a few or be pushed off, but I'd get back inside—I'm swinging without stop—most guys couldn't stay with me. Earl had fought pro in the ring. He was my trainer, taught me how to hook to the head, how to finish a cat when you hurt him. I took a few guys out and my rep was made. Like Earl used to say, "Don't mess with Hoppy." Being Earl was smarter than me, I'd listen to him. He'd come on with, "Look here, Holmes, you got to dig yo'self—you gonna be on the street soon, forget about that okey-doke shit—gorilla-ing people, robbing pads—the shit is on, Briss, I got the word from Rocco—the junk is already here. And we is in—you think some guinea is going up to 125th and Lenox to deal with the niggers or to 111th and Fifth to deal with the spics? They gonna need distributors with brains and with heart—stand-up motherfuckers. I don't know about you, but I'm declaring myself in. These wops don't fuck around, bro—you got to play with their rules. Your word is your life—they make a meet, be there! This Mickey Mouse jive with the pussy and the coke and the booze don't mean nothin'. Got to be cool, stay clean. Make the move a few times a year—that's it. After a while, I'll have my own crew—then I'm gonna make my own world. I ain't gonna be a nigger all my life, pushing wooden Cadillacs on 37th Street—not Mrs. Bassey's boy. I'm going all the way—they got to kill me, Jack, kill me!"

"What about me, Earl, what about me?"

"You gonna be my man with the Ricans, Chappie—they ain't nothing but niggers turned inside out."

Rocco was from another garage—but a boss-type. Tall, lean, with light hair, he didn't look like no eye-talian to me. And he didn't give you the wise-guy jive. He was mobbed up with the Pleasant Avenue outfit. But his uncle was a made-guy, a lieutenant with the Mulberry Street crew—a heavy hitter—so like you knew that Rocco was marked. He couldn't miss, he was a down cat, and he was connected. Rocco didn't talk with no *dese* and *dose;* he spoke nice and soft—like dignity—but he wasn't no punk. Word was he had already iced some greaseball in the Bronx whose bail had dropped too low. The only thing wrong with Rocco was his love life; he had this thing for a P.R. chick, which in those days was unheard of, so like his uncle kept him in the boondocks—but I knew he'd work it out. Like I say, he was a natural boss-type.

The three of us used to pal out. They'd rap and I'd listen.

"Earl, I'm out of the doghouse, so I'll be moving downtown—you know where to reach me. I'm not promising you guys anything, but if I get a shot then I'm dealing you in. We may connect once in a year, or even five years—in the meantime I don't even know if you guys are alive. We meet, we deal, good-bye. Now I'm not talking Harlem shit, I'm talking kilos, up to ten thou a kilo. On my okay you're going to get stuff on consignment at the beginning. You cross me, I'm dead, because I'm responsible for you—but you know you go right behind me. I'm moving up; you guys can move with me or stay in the shithouse hustling quarters."

"I'm your man, Rocco."

"Deal me in, Rocco."

It's hard to explain, but when you're doing time with a man you can read him faster than when you're on the street. He can't hide behind his rep or his clothes—shit like that don't work inside. Inside, all you got is mostly yourself. Like Earl used to say, yo' hole and yo' soul is buck neck-id in the Joint. So that's how come three cats from different alleys got close and stayed close for twenty years. The time was ripe, was overdue—but that don't mean nothin' if the right people ain't on the scene. Me and Earl was the right people, and we was ready. We needed a break. Rocco—Rocco had the inside rail from before, what with his uncle, Dominick Cocozza, who was a boss. But he saw their thing had to open up—open up or it was gonna bust open.

So he brought us in out of the rain. He didn't do it overnight, 'specially for me; I was still a cowboy for years yet. But I knew he knew I was stand-up, and later than sooner he would cut me loose into the big bucks. Earl first, then me. Rocco was the icebreaker and he done the right thing. And it took balls, because there was fool wops that couldn't see it—no put grits, rice, and beans in the pasta. Prejudiced old fucks like Rocco's boss, Pete Amadeo (*maldita sea su madre*), who thought they could sit inside the one tent with a whole bunch of Indians like me and Earl runnin' around outside bare-ass in the cold. Not to forget the hole the feds was diggin' under the floor.

Sick—some of them guys is sick too. You take Amadeo—a/k/a Petey A. One night at the Copa—this is when Tom Jones was at his peak. All the wise guys 'n dolls was jammed in—place was hysteria. Broads throwin' their keys, their drawers even, at Jones. Pete says to this button-guy with him,

"He's a fuckin' nigger. All this noise over a fuckin' nigger."

"No, Pete, you got it wrong—he's English."

"I say he's a fuckin' nigger, awright?"

"Eh, yeah, you're right, Pete—lookit the way he dances."

We split from the El in the order we came in. First Rocco, then Earl, then me. I hit Harlem like Sonny hit Floyd.

2

THE FIFTIES CAME IN STRONG FOR ME. LIKE DANCE-CRAZY.
The St. Nick's Arena, the Manhattan Center, the Caborojeño, Broadway Casino—seems like everybody was
dancing their ass off. The tigers would go to the Cabo
and the BC, the down P.R.'s would go to the Palladium.
The Manhattan Center would be the place for Easter,
maybe six bands followed by a riot where 3 or 4 guys
would be thrown off the balcony. One Easter was maybe
two hundred cats rumbling, tables crashing, bottles flying, and in the middle of this Noro Morales on the band-
stand, "Pliz, we all Puerto Rican pipples, no fight. . . ." I
laughed so hard I could hardly swing my chair.

The bands were hot—Machito, Puente, Rodriguez,
Curbelo, Marcelino Guerra, they was all gigging.

The main joint was the Palladium on 53rd Street and
Broadway; the owner was a Jew named Max, but if you
looked around you knew he had friends. All the help was

27

wops. The bouncers were somethin' else—real class. Like some *jíbaro* would throw a right hand; they'd catch his fist in midair, lift him off his feet, his little shoes kicking in the air, rush him to the back door parallel to the ground like a torpedo; a bouncer had the door ready— he's gone, head-first down a flight of concrete steps. The dancers wouldn't even break stride.

But the house wouldn't fuck with the wise-guys. We brought in the bread, drank J & B, had the sharp broads. Lots of dressing in those days—dark suits, roll collars, skinny silk ties, short hair—dap as a Russian pimp. Fridays was our night. All the hustlers were there—l03rd Street, 106th, 107th, 111th, 116th—Mario, Guajiro, Toñin, Cano. Everybody was cool—except maybe if the Viceroys and the Turbens was there on the same night. I would back out then because I was tight with both clicks and couldn't take sides when they'd get it on.

I always had my table with my own crew, Tato and Victor Lopez, Lalin, Monkey, Colorado—salty mother-fuckers all. I was the main man. None of us was too smart then, but my hands were the best and in them days there was still duking with the fists, at least among the spics. We was small-timing in them days—thievery, nickel bags, and strong arm.

The broads were all over; we'd team up mostly with whores. Who else is going to snort coke with you in an after-hours joint or see you go for a yard when your bread is down? My old lady then was India from 113th Street; she was underage and her mother was going to lock me up, but after the kid was born we was okay. She was the most beautiful *mulata* uptown but she had this thing about being white—kept talking about the kid having good hair. P.R.'s used to make a big thing about hair in them days—this guy's got good hair, this guy bad, this guy suspicious hair. Me, I never gave a fuck—guess I was ahead of my time.

Mainly India was good people, but she was just a kid and very wacky. Like we'd be comin' out of a restaurant with some people and she'd jump on my back—"Carlito, carry me piggyback." 'Ey, I was already a mature cat—done time—respected. India's mother didn't go for me; I was a thug. Meanwhile, I know for a fact the old lady used to turn tricks in her day—had a fine body just like the daughter. All them "India" broads got fine bodies. Anyway, we didn't last long. The two of them and the baby, a girl, Prudencia (that was the grandmother's name), ended up in Florida with some Air Force guy India married. She had some shape, India did—like a guitar. You knew someday she was gonna turn into a bull fiddle, but in the meantime—some good strummin', Jack. Believe that.

Wednesdays was celebrity night at the Palladium—all the showbiz and Jews doing cha-cha-cha-one-two-three, Marlon Brando sit in on conga (couldn't play to save his ass), out-of-town people—shit like that—all into Latin music. I say that put the spics on the map; we wasn't all behind them little glass panes at Horn & Hardart. Yeah, like a P.R. pot washer could dance up a storm at the Palladium and walk out some fine out-of-town fox. Yeah, the old P was all right. Had a hell of a run too. The forties, the fifties, right up to the early sixties. Then some lame was puffing on a joint one night, got next to a kitty and said she had to take a poke. In them days mari-gee-wana was a big deal. The broad blew up, ran downtown and put the squeal on the Palladium to her boss, an assistant D.A. name of Kuh who was already into being one of Hogan's main honchos. So now you got shoo-fly checking out the P and first thing down is a pimp name of Umberto beating up on two of his whores. And what does they see the house do? Throw the broads down the stairs and buy Umberto a drink. This is an outrage, say Mr. Kuh. And the great Palladium raid was on. 'Cept that by that time all the heavy people knew it was coming off—yeah, stool pigeons fly in both directions. So like, block all the exits, blow all the lights—"Everybody freeze!" By the time they got the lights back on, all the guns, knives, and dope was on the floor and the bulls was running around trying to match up whozis with whatzis. It was a jive raid but it blew the liquor license and the old P went under. Damn shame. Somebody always gotta mess up a good thing.

MIDWAY UP THE FIFTIES, EARL BASSEY SENT WORD HE wanted a meet with me. I'd run into Earl from time to time; I knew he was big in policy up in black Harlem. Sunday night at the Copa: I knew right away we was connected. So the wops are cutting loose; they been hog-

ging it all to themselves—finally giving the natives a
break. I got myself all dolled up and went down—big
night at the Copa. The boys was all in their tiers, according to rank. Cigars, white-on-white, pinkie rings—the
broads, roamin' noses, with hair teased like brillo. Every
table like a little click, with the boss playing his crew like
he had a baton—he laughs, they laugh, he gets up, they
get up.

"So I sez to him. . . ."

"*Madon'*, Fonso, you got some pair of balls. . . ."

"He's a fuckin' *cafone*. . . ."

I don't see a black face in the whole joint. I go back
upstairs to the lounge and order a drink. I ain't there five
minutes when there's a big commotion coming up from
downstairs. This little blond guy is raising hell—he's got
three or four guys with him, spitters all—the maitre d' is
pleading, "Please Joey, please!"

"I wanna see this Jew cocksucker right here and now!"

This little Jew comes off the bar.

"What's the trouble, Joey?"

"What's the trouble? What kind of ratjoint is this that
I got to sit in the back—I don't rate around here? Where's
my respect?"

"Joey, please—there's been a mixup with the tables,
we'll straighten it out—"

By this time, this Joey guy is stone-white in the face.
He whips out an automatic and starts banging it on top
of the bar—splinters flying—he's screaming, "I'm gonna
shylock this joint, I am in—starting next week you're
turning over to me—you hear, you Jew bastard?"

"Whatever you say, Joey, whatever you say." The Jew was cool, ice water. Sweat was coming down my spine; other people's beefs always scare me more than my own. I never seen such a show of *cojones;* there was a hundred guys frozen there—half of them had to be packing.

Then they were gone. About that time Earl came in—clean as always. He had with him a high-yaller chick that wouldn't quit. Uuwee!

I was still shook up. I told him this wop Joey, from Brooklyn, had terrorized the joint. Earl said, "He be bad as ten sacks of motherfuckers, but he ain't coming back next week; he's crazy, but he ain't that crazy."

This guy comes over and says to us, "You're Mr. Fabrizi's guests?" Well all right!

Rocco, you sombitch, I knew you was heavy in the mambo when I saw that table right down on the floor. Some mobbed-up Jew comedian was on the floor and every joke was played to some capo at ringside, like "Sonny this" and "Sonny that." I knew enough not to want to know who these guys were, but I was impressed—heavy, heavy.

About this time, slipping and sliding, Mr. Rocco Fabrizi. He looked like money—tiny cuff links, tiny watch, shoulders just right on the suit. Rimless glasses in them days, warm smile—the guy could get to you.

"Did you marry her?"

"Yes, Charles, I am now a Puerto Rican by proxy."

We were bullshitting awhile about upstate when Earl sent his broad upstairs.

"Let's hear the deal."

"Charles, there's a West Indian guy named Etienne uptown who's got a nice little policy bank going for many years. This guy is right next to Earl here. But lately we feel he's loosening up, getting old. Now there are some boys up there eyeballing old Etienne and they are ready to bite. What we need is somebody to prop old Etienne up for a while, keep the wolves at bay and then when things are ripe ease him out to pasture. Earl says you're the man."

"That's great and I can handle it, but why not take the old fart out right now?"

"No good; Etienne has run a good bank since the thirties. People trust him; you can't remove him overnight—this will be done our way."

"Whatever you guys say."

So now me and my boys were riding shotgun for old Etienne. We'd wake him up and put him to bed. He took a liking to me, and we'd rap in Spanish; he was a Haitian but he spoke Spanish, English, and French. That smart old geezer owned buildings, dry cleaning stores, groceries, you name it. But policy was his game—he was a genius at that. He knew all the dream books by heart, the Chinaman in the *Daily News;* he knew just when to lay off on certain numbers—it's like he would sense a heavy hit coming—like the plate numbers on a car in the newspaper or in a plane crash. He would start his own rumors about a special number being fixed for the controllers to hit—all his own bullshit—but he was always cooking; he'd stake people who needed money, helped a whole lot of people and he always paid his hits, no hedging. I learned a lot from him, old Etienne.

Right away I started earning my keep. The old man had the hots for some barmaid in the Heights in a joint called Carl's Corner. He dug that young poontang—even though at his age I knew he was shooting blanks. So like I was downtown in a bar when I get a call from this guy Snipe—"Carlito, they got Mr. Etienne in the back of a short in front of Carl's."

"Cops?"

"Club members, with a sawed-off shotgun in his face; they want twenty large right away."

"I'll be right there."

Maso the bartender loaned me this army .45, plus I had my own .32 Beretta automatic. I cocked both pieces and jumped in a cab. I got off at 149th and Broadway—they was double-parked in front of the joint, first in line facing uptown. I come from behind on the outside; I shove both automatics through the rear window, right in this guy's face—two spades, one shotgun, the old man between them.

"Make your move, motherfucker, make it—"

"Whoa, bro—"

"I'll splash your face all over this motherfuckin' car—"

"You right, man, you right."

The old man got out okay. But his nerves were bad after that. He said I was crazy, but it wasn't like that. I just didn't give a fuck; got a beef, jump out in front; you be first, you be best.

We checked Snipe out; he was wrong—set Etienne up. Somebody burnt some holes in his clothes. Later for Snipe.

ABOUT THAT TIME THE OLD MAN STARTED STAYING AT home in St. Albans. That was all right with me. Good bread coming in. Everything copasetic. Too good to last. I started moving around more. Had me over twenty suits, three hundred a pop, from Leighton's, Cye Martin, and Kronfeld's. All my boys stayed clean; we'd run down to Atlantic City—Club Harlem, 500 Club—even Miami and Puerto Rico—we'd have parties with five or six broads snorting coke and doing tricks. I started going to the Copa regular; if I caught the show always a yard for the maitre d'—"Mr. Brigante, right this way." I was palling around with a lot of wops from downtown and the west Bronx, younger guys like me, not the prejudiced old hoods. These kids would say I was half a wop with my name, which is Corsican—of which there's a lot in P.R. I'd think, maybe I'm gonna be the first made-guy P.R., and I'd say, *"Fangul"* and "Yer mudder's cunt" with the best of them. I shoulda known better.

Earl would come down when he had something to say to Rocco. Neither one of them would party as much as me. And they'd be down on me for fuckin' around so much. I'd listen,'cause I knew these cats was in my corner, but I couldn't see it. When you're highrollin' in the bread you're bound to be out there jumpin' come midnight every night. Rocco and Earl was businessmen, while-as I was a jive-ass party man. But I'd complain anyway.

"Rocco, gimme a break. Earl, here, be a doctor of numerology, like Etienne. But numbers ain't my game, Rocco. I ain't got the patience. Gimme a break."

"He wants to be the main skag man uptown, Rocco. He think he can fuck with the feds."

"Charles, you've been handed a ready-made, going concern. Etienne has the best runners in Harlem."

"Yeah, but I gotta work every day. Somebody's always trying to sneak in a late hit or change a number on us. Then you gotta be an administrator; then you got labor problems—what controller is humpin' what runner's wife. Rocco, I'm breakin' my ass."

"The money's good, right?"

"Slow comin'."

"What do you think, Earl?"

"Carlito's okay, Rocco. The bank's holdin' up."

"Okay, Mister Carlito. Next time I have an auction you may be invited."

"I'm ready, Rocco, I'm ready."

"Paint is very expensive, maybe ten thou for a bucket."

"Money is only an object, I'll get it. Got it, been there. Wadda you kiddin', I been waiting since we left the El, Rocco. Right, Earl?"

"I got no beef with the policy game, Carlito. Since Rocco got me on the pad, I been straight. Numbers is hard work, but it's clean. That don't mean I won't take a shot if I get a chance. Meantime I'm cool."

"Junk shakes you up, eh, Earl?"

"Earl is smart, Charles; he leaves well enough alone.
He gets up early, he works hard, he sleeps nights. This
other business is like Grand Prix racing. You have to keep
your hands on the wheel at all times. You get the best
engineers, the best mechanics, the best car, and they'll
still run you into a wall. I don't recommend it to anybody. You're on a different level in that game—the air
is very thin. You can choke on it."

"When did you ever know me to take a step back,
Rocco?"

"It's not that, I don't want later on—"

"Rocco, I'm ready, gimme a break."

"Take care of things uptown, with Earl here; later on,
we'll see."

Meanwhile, uptown some dudes is getting jealous—
spics is like that. I'm tooling around in a big car with a
fine kitty. Instead of saying one of the boys made it, no,
they got to get mad; that jive Carlito, he ain't shit,
when's the last time he took to the street with a cat—
they wuz gonna try me out again. Mistake! It came
down this way. I had me a fabulous Jewish chick name
of Honey, a stone freak. A blonde, educated too—but
she dug wise-guys. I'd play the Little Caesar shit for
her and she loved it. She'd even come up to Harlem to
meet me. One night she was waiting for me in this joint
near 111th Street and Fifth Avenue. These three kiddie
hoodlums came in, grabbed her fur coat right off her
back.

"Tell Carlito that Chucho wants to see him; we'll hold
your coat."

They were gone when I got there—lucky for me, since I didn't have no piece on me. The broad was all shook up. I told Guiso, the owner of the joint, "Tell Chucho I'll see him tomorrow night right here. I'm very embarrassed about my fiancée's coat—make sure he brings the coat; we'll work something out." Well all right. Step right up.

I dug the whole scene, that's my trouble. I coulda had these punks taken out—no, I wanna do it myself; my blood was hot, got to be my hands.

It was after midnight, the three of them was in the joint facing the door, the fur coat thrown over a chair, I had a long leather coat on with a pistol in each pocket—automatics can jam, but they're faster. Only one way in or out to Guiso's diner, no back door. I come in the door smilin'—"*Ola,* Chucho"—then I started smoking with both pieces; Chucho said, "*Espera,* Carlito . . . ," that's as far as he got. We were going to talk all right. I killed him standing up. His partner, Nelson, took two in the chest—he had something on him, but he never got off. The third guy split out the door, taking tables with him; I chased him past the Park Palace into the park but he was movin', Jim!—he got away. I come back for the coat—some motherfucker had copped it. I come out and see Nelson crawling under a parked car—I bent down and put another cap in him—he screamed like a pussy. I quit the scene in a hurry.

Now I was in a real jackpot. Everything was fucked up. Why I got to be such a hothead? I blow town, get upstate around Newburgh. Earl, my man, come up to see me.

"Rocco be hot as a motherfucker about you, bro. He say you done blown the whole duke. He's right. That macho shit of yours shows you ain't no boss. Three street punks. You coulda skinned them cats twenty different ways without—"

"Had to be, Earl, it was coming—I just got off first. What's to be?"

"Cuba, Carlito."

"Cuba, what the hell I'm gonna do in Cuba?"

"Lay cool—you're driving down to Miami, then take the ferry to Havana. Rocco's sending a guy named Vinnie to pick you up; he'll have the other half of this dollar bill on him. Watch the speed limits driving down. When you get to Havana he'll connect you—you be there awhile; when things calm down here, Rocco will send for you."

"Wait a minute, Earl, I got a self-defense case here. I can beat this in court tell Rocco to get me Murray or Kleinman—"

"How you sound? That Nelson punk is alive, a material witness with $100,000 bail. Now how we know if he's gonna stand up? Gotta get that bail down, then we know what he's told the D.A. If push come to shove, we can wash him—but right now you need time, get it, time!"

"What about the other kids?"

"Chucho's underground; the third guy is still runnin' through the park—don't worry about them."

"Well then, we go to Cuba."

This guy Vinnie shows up next day, the dollar halves match, and we're off in a Caddie, and I mean off, this

dude wouldn't sleep or talk—a driving sphinx. In twenty
hours we're in north Florida. We're humming on an
empty stretch of highway when there they were in the
rearview mirror. Bulls. They pull us over.

Storm troops. Six-foot-two and twice as wide and as
mean as they was wide. Wide-brimmed hats, pearl-
handled revolvers—they must still be killing Indians
around here.

"License and registration."

"Yes, sir," says Vinnie, showing his license. We're
both out of the Caddie.

"Dagos, eh, drivin' a big Cadillac from the big city—
where yo'all barrel-assing to?"

Oh shit.

"We're going to Miami, sir," says Vinnie—but the
more you give the more they push.

"All you ginsos is comin' to Miami and Tampa—"

"I'm Spanish"—I'm hot.

"You ain't nothin' but a Cuban nigger—"

I threw a short right hand just below the breastbone—
he went down on his ass, cowboy shit and all. He'd have
shot me for sure but his partner stopped him. They handcuffed and slapped us around. Then they took us to a
diner on the road; the cook took his apron off and come
out as the fucking magistrate. The bulls told him what
happened.

"Good Godalmighty damn, cain't decent folks be on
our roads without gittin' run over with these heah big
cars? Ah swear, it's a goddamn shame—an' now they
wanna be assaulting peace officers. Couple of may-fia

boys, eh? Wal, that don' cut no ice 'round heah; we'll put yo' ass on the chain gang, yo'all heah, the chain gang."

If he was trying to scare me, he sure as hell was succeeding—I was scared shitless.

"Yeah, you lil' ol' boys are in trouble—serious trouble. Now, whut kind of car was that? A Cadillac, eh? Lemme talk to the driver. Take this heah other boy out."

They took me to a back room. My ass was low—I'll be breaking rocks in a chain gang and if I'm lucky the warrant will come down on the N.Y. homicide.

After a while, Vinnie came to get me with the bulls; they drove us to a bus depot. Not a word was said. Then they put Vinnie and me on a bus headed for Miami.

"The man wanted the car?"

"Yeah."

"Man got the car?"

"Yeah." End of conversation.

3

Havana was really jumping in those days—best town I was ever in. Tropicana, Montmartre, with chorus lines of *mulatas* that put anything in N.Y. to shame. You could party twenty-four hours a day—Olga Guillot, Benny More, Rolando La Serie, they were all there. La Aragon, Casino la Playa, Cascarita—gambling, pussy, coke—wide open. Fidel sure fucked up a good thing.

The mob was into all the casinos and I was hanging around the tables a lot. Pretty soon I teamed up with this Cuban named Nacho Reyes. He was the bodyguard for a senator and had connections all the way to the president. The setup was different there; every politico had his own crew working for him—like private little armies. Everybody was robbing, but you had to be in the government, so at election time things would get rough; murders were all right as long as you had your rabbi—cops and robbers were all mixed up. If your man was in

you were a cop, uniform and all—if not, you'd be a rob-
ber trying to get him in. Wild.

Nacho was a stone killer, he iced a guy when he was
sixteen years old and kept right on going. He had bullet holes all over his body. I never saw him eat anything,
but he would snort coke day and night. With a piece in
his hand he was like a cat, a bad-ass. He said he had
heard about me in New York—that I had *cojones*. I
learned a lot from Nacho. One night we walked into this
joint and right away I could see it was a setup. The door
was closed behind us, the jukebox was loud—the bartender looked like he was going to start crying. The hairs
on the back of my neck said, "These motherfuckers are
going to kill us."

Nacho saved our ass. He threw his arms around the
bossman there—"*Mi hermano,* I have come to your
house to have a drink with you as your guest; Carlito
from New York, I have spoken to him about our Cuban
hospitality . . ."

Nacho ate crow but he saved our lives. After we left,
he said, "Only a fool throws himself head first—when
you are outgunned and your only exit is death, you com-
promise; *le comes el cerebro,* when the time is right, you
strike—but you never hesitate. That is why I am alive
and have buried a dozen men. The coke is in my nose
but not my brain—"

I WAS IN CUBA FOR OVER A YEAR HAVING A HIGH OLD TIME.
I was in a beach club, had a Cuban old lady—Earl would

send me money when I needed it. My *Cubana* was a hooker, but she was a classy broad and moved in good circles. She spoke very refined Spanish and had elegant hands—I'd forget she was turnin' tricks. She'd tell me how great I was, how I wasn't cut out to be a knock-around guy. She was going to con a con man. Ha!

Then I got the word from Earl. Everything is set, come on home. *Adiós, Cubita la bella.*

I surrendered to the D.A.'s office accompanied by my lawyer, Morris Steinhardt. They took me to the sixth floor, Homicide Bureau, for interrogation before arraignment. They got to be kidding. They questioned me in teams, the first team was threatening me, hooping and hollering; the second team was going to save me from the first, only I got to tell them the truth about the murder. Name and address, that's all they get.

I'm arraigned in Central Sessions that afternoon. Murder in the first degree; I could get the electric chair, Jesus! No bail, they hold me in the Tombs. Tombs is right—couldn't take a shower, place smells bad, food worse.

The word is that I am in good shape—all they got is a bus driver who says he saw me chasing a guy into the park with something in my hand but he's not sure what. Guiso's going to say he saw me around his joint that night but didn't see me at the time of the shooting and that he dove to the floor without looking as soon as he heard the first bang. The guns were never found and to add to the confusion, ballistics is going to show Chucho and Nelson were shot with different guns, like there was more than one guy shooting. They got no statement out of me since I come in with my lawyer. Earl tells me that Nelson is all right—he don't know who did what, all he knows he was shot. I don't go for this, I say wash Nelson, but Rocco says it will look bad, so I go along with them.

Meanwhile, I got troubles with my fuckin' lawyer. He's getting big bucks and he ain't doing shit. I got to lead him by the hand all the way. They are like these doctors who ask you what's wrong with you; if you know, what the hell you need them for? Shit. I break it all down for the lawyer—all the motions I want made—I want all the statements from all the witnesses, I want the ballistics reports, I want the autopsy report. I want the yellow sheets on all the prosecution witnesses, I want the case dismissed for lack of prosecution—the lawyer says that ain't got no merit 'cause I ran away. Ran away, shit, who ran away? I wasn't there, I just went to Cuba for a vacation—and if I was there I ran away from the same gang of guys that shot Chucho and Nelson, I ran for my life. This old con Walter, down from Dannemora on his own writ, told me what I had to do. He should know, he's been drawing writs for twenty years.

Me and Walter got together and wrote a summation for my case. Walter would sound off in the tank,

"Ladeez and genulmens of the ju-ree, yo'all is here to dee-termine iffen dis here boy be innercent or he be guilty. Now you got to know that this be important to the dee-fendant—now right away the Dee Ay gonna say that the case is important to the peoples too. Now what kind of nonsense is that? The peoples cain't go to jail, the peoples cain't go to the 'lectric chair, is only this here boy can go—so damn sho' more important to him! The judge he gonna tell you about reasonable doubts—ah say ain't no reason to doubt that this boy be innercent. Ain't no haps here, ain't even *per*haps. Now what went down here—I'm gonna tell yo'all.

"De deceased, may his soul rest in peace, he were a villain—he done been busted for everythin' in the book—assault, robbery, burglary, dope, and even un-lawful entry on a young lady. He weren't nothin' but a dirty dawg. He was uptown—whut wuz he doin' up-town? I'll tell you whut—he was gorillaing peoples, mugging peoples—innercent hardwerking peoples like the defendant—that' whut he was doing. Ain't nobody gonna miss that mother—I'm gonna say it—that Chucho deserved killin'. That don't mean the defendant killed him, but he deserved it. Now the Dee Ay gonna say my man here killed Chucho. That be a dirty lie. Iffen he was there he didn't kill no Chucho, and ah ain't sayin' he was there—iffen he was there he was runnin' fo' dear life—they was shootin' goin' on in that joint— yessir, Chucho'll tell you that—whut's a man to do but run? Sheet, ah hear pop, pop, mah feet gonna run right out from under me. You people got to hip up that this weren't no Waldorf-Astoria, this were Harlem—it's mean out there. Now Guiso, he didn't see nuthin', he hit the dirt—I don't blame him, but you think iffen he saw who shot up his customers he wouldn' say? Damn right he would, but he ain't gonna lie—he don't know. Ballistics, what did they say? They didn't say nuthin' 'cept that they was two guns used—who was the defendant then? Wild Bill Hickok or Wyatt Herp with two guns? You gotta know there was a whole lot of guns there—and what about Chucho and Nelson, what was they packin'? It weren't no parcel post—and what about this third dude whut got away—where is he? where is he? That be the mystery here—why the Dee Ay don't bring him here, where he hidin', why he hidin'? Go to China, Dee Ay gonna find ya—go to Mangolia, Dee Ay gonna find ya—go to Spotsylvania, Dee Ay gonna find ya—meanwhile he cain't find this dude whut was seen runnin' in the park. That park ain't so big—he got to come out sometime—somebody's jiving.

"And the cops in this case—what did they tell you? That mah man come in under his own voluntary—yessuh, he come in under his own ree-cognizance—he was outa town on business awhile when he heard the law was looking for him and he come right on in. Ain't no lammister here—he here to face the charges. Les talk about this here Nelson—you saw him slippin', slidin', and glidin' here, didn't you? Ooweee—what a dirty dawg! Talk about stealin' a hot stove, this turkey will steal the stove, the pots, the pans, and the dirty underwear. It's a dirty shame the Dee Ay with all his money got to bring in such a no-account witness—ah gets sick in mah stomach thinking about that Nelson—pardon me while I drink some water. That man would deal in confederate money—a menace to chillun and society.

"You saw him up there on the stand sashaying around—no shave, no tie—he ain't got no respect for this courtroom. I'm gonna let you in on somethin'. You want to know who the killer is, you really want to know who the killer is? Don't look no further than that Nelson. There he be, brazen as all git-out, with the mark of Cain on him, and he ain't even got no tie on—whereupon look at mah man here—clean, respetable, white shirt and tie. That ain't no killer sitting there, thas' a Po' Rican there, and thas why he's there. Everytime somethin' happen uptown the po-lice run out and grab the first Po' Rican or nigro they can get their hands on. Pre-judice is heah, yes it is.

"Ladeez and genulmens of the ju-ree, it come to me last night when I was thinking what I am going to tell them intelligent peoples on that ju-ree—yessuh, I do believe the good Lord in his infinite wisdom, he done shot it down to me as I lay there thinking, and here's whut I heard: this here Nelson and Chucho had a shoot-out between them, thas why each was shot with bullets from different guns; they collapsed and a thief ran away with both guns. Why, thas plain as can be. Now ah know ah ain't no Clarence Darrence, but that don't mean ah ain't telling it like it is. You gotta go in the ju-ree room and argue and you gotta cut this man loose, 'cause he ain't hurt nobody! Now, the law give the Dee Ay the last word—that ain't right, but thas the law. But never mind whut he say, you remember whut ah tol' yo'all, 'cause thas where it's at."

About that time I'd file in like I was the foreman of the jury and ol' black Walter would say, "Mr. Foreman, has the ju-rcc rcached a verdict yet?"

I'd say, "We have, Your Honor."

"And what is your verdict?"

I'd say, "Not guilty on all counts, and now we want to lock up all the lying motherfuckers the D.A. put on the stand." Had a lot of fun with Walter.

THE REAL THING WENT DOWN DIFFERENT. THE SOMBITCH lawyer Steinhardt didn't cross-examine Nelson right. On direct examination by the D.A., Nelson said he didn't see who it was that shot him and Chucho. That ain't good enough—he got to say no, that ain't the man; otherwise with the other shit thrown in I'm gonna get tagged. Now Nelson wants to do the right thing, but the D.A. has him scared. All Steinhardt has to do is lead him over the hurdles to "No, that ain't the man," but he don't know how to do it. First, he loves the sound of his own voice rolling all the r's, then he don't never use two syllables where six will do. He wants to know about wind velocity, about one foot from the door and was the doorknob on the left or the right; did the guy put his left foot in front of his right or his right in front of his left? And every time Steinhardt gets an answer to his stupid-ass questions he looks at the jury like, "Aha!" Well, by the time Steinhardt got through with Nelson, whatever the D.A. left out Steinhardt filled in. So we ended up with Nelson saying "I don't know who," and

I was in trouble. I couldn't get on the stand because of my record and all the shit they might bring out.

The jury hung up. I made bail then and went back to the street. I was just getting back into the groove when Steinhardt calls me up.

"Manslaughter in the first degree with a ceiling of five."

"A pound—that's too much, counselor."

"D.A. says he's got a line on that third guy you chased."

"He's bluffing."

"Maybe so, but you're in no position to take chances; this is a P-and-D murder rap—there can be no recommendation of mercy."

"Let me think about it."

What was there to think about? I copped. The night before I went in we had a big party at the Copa. All the boys were there. Everybody was stoned—nearly everybody. Rocco pulled me aside—"Don't feel too bad about going in, Charles, it's only a couple of years. Keep your nose clean and when you come out you can get next to me. It's taken me a few years, but now I'm ready. This rule about the junk is not for me. The bosses are sitting on millions and they say, you no do-a this, you no do-a that—meanwhile they close the books and the soldiers have to drive trucks on the side to live.

"I've told them, there's a demand, there must be a supply—we step out, somebody else will step in. We can't afford that, matter of economics. All the soldiers in all the gambling and shylocking don't compare to what a few guys can do with junk. There's just no comparison. I was in Europe and my setup is complete over there. Over here I've had some trial runs with my boss—so far, okay; he turns his head away—except when I put the money in his hand, then he looks real hard. Of course, if anything happens, I'm dead—but that's all right—a little balls, a little brains, that's all you need. Why am I telling you this, Charles? Because I want you to go in knowing there's a big place waiting for you when you come out. You've stood up under some bad breaks and you've learned how to take orders—I want you by my side."

I was approaching my thirties, about time my train came in.

Upstate. I went first to Ossining, then to Green Haven. The whole neighborhood was up there. All junkies stealing to support their habit. Seemed like all of a sudden everyone was on junk. Got to be crazy, sticking that shit in their veins. Not crazy, just weak—and a bunch of them support one strong guy, that's the law of nature. Big fish eat a whole lot of little fish, and one lion eats twenty zebras. Everyone down on the pusher, but he don't push nobody, he only push the dope. He provides a service, that's all—somebody got to do it. Somebody wants something, somebody else gonna step out and get it for him—he got to be paid for that, that's the way it's always been. As for me, if they're gonna give me my druthers, I'd druther be a fucker than a fuckee.

In the Joint I always get in top shape; no coke, no pot, no pussy, so you work out. I always do good time—I don't go 'round whining about how I got framed again. I'm a *hodedor* and I'm paying some of my dues. If I'm dressing out of Leighton's and driving Caddies and Lincolns, there got to be a tab sometime; I got no time for these chumps crying about how they never had no chance 'cause their mammy was a whore or their daddy was a lush—who wants to hear that shit? You wanna be a hoodlum, be a pro; if you can't take the time, don't do the crime.

All these shrink and psycho mumbo-jumbo artists is making good money on these prison staffs and they don't know shit. This here's a capitalist country, ain't it? Which means supply-and-demand and dog-eat-dog. First is best and fuck the rest. I'll buy that, I'll compete—but on my terms. I'll go for the goodies, but I can't compete with my brains or family or education, so I do it with my balls. I'll take a shot where most people will step back. But if I come out the other side then I want a bigger cut of the pie—that's the dues the system got to pay. Ain't no mafia in China, but who wants to walk around in pajamas—see what I mean?

That's the kind of shit that goes down in the Joint—three years I had to hear it. Who got twenty whores and three Lincolns on the street? All the rice-and-beans pimps. And who's got the pipeline to the main man in France? All the nickel-and-dime bag-pushers. The criminal mind is a bitch. I don't want nothing to do with these scumbags; I know where I'm going and it don't include none of them. I'm with them but I ain't into them.

Then there's the sex problem in the Joint. When you're in, the worst skank you ever had becomes like a movie star. I've heard guys talk about streetwalkers as "the

mother of my children" and "mi señora." Unbelievable.
But a whole lot of suffering behind that shit too—I seen
stone killers cry on a Christmas or New Year's, I seen a
made-guy turn his head to a wall and will himself to death
'cause his old lady left him for another guy. Me, I don't
give a fuck. I stay loose at all times, travel light—always
been like that ever since I hit the street, age twelve. Then
you got the faggots. Bad news. Once a guy starts on that
you got to put him down—pretty soon you don't know
who's the poger and who's the pogee.

And you get the legal faculty cons. Writing coram
nobis and habeas corpses up the ass, arguing cases like
they was Earl Warren. If you so slick, why you here,
motherfucker? Get out my face.

Least, but not last, you got the stool pigeons. They go
'round dropping kites on everybody. Like:

Chief Judge
Court of Appeals
Federal Courthouse
Foley Square, New York

Your Honor:
On April 1, 1918, at 8:43 A.M. I saw Joe Bacia-
galupe sell to Joe Abafangul a kilo of smack. I
would be happy to testify about the herein incident.
So far the five county D.A.'s, the U.S. Attorney,
and the Attorney General have refused to act on
my complaint. But I got something on them too. I
know you ain't on the take so I'll expect to hear

from you soon. All I'm asking is consideration on my fourth felony which I got a bum rap on account of a stool pigeon name of Joe Ugatz.

> Your friend,
> Louis Linguini

P.S. I'm sending a copy of this letter to your boss in Wash., D.C.

or

District Attorney
New York County
New York, New York

Your Honor:

On July 4, 1902, my then lawyer, Oscar Meyer, gave to Det. McNulty of the 32 the sum of $500 to beat my case. Meanwhile I'm still here. This is an outrage and I demand to be called as a witness. My time is your time.

> Sincerely,
> R.A. Fink

P.S. I'm sending a copy of this letter to Morris Nadjari.

WHEN A GUY GOES BAD, HE'S A RENEGADE, BECAUSE HE'S already lined up against society and now he's going against his own kind. He's in no-man's-land—and like the guys in no-man's-land, he's supposed to get killed. Unless he's ratting on the Latins or the Blacks—then if he survives the first twenty-four hours, he's all right; he can sit ringside at the Chateau Madrid or Smalls, 'cause the spooks and the spics can only stay mad twenty-four hours, then they forget—jive-ass. But the wops can stay mad a long time—one guy's supposed to have been done under ten years later when he got spotted as an extra in some flick—ten years he'd been cool on the West Coast. I heard of spitters going down to Honduras and Panama to ice a rat. Now that's staying mad! With the spics, if a stoolie moves from 111th Street to the Bronx he's out of the jurisdiction—jive-ass. That's why they all be in Lewisburg or Green Haven. Wise up, turkey.

If you been in the slams one time, you been in all of them, but if you're gonna survive in there, you got to be cool. Your rep gets there before you do, but you got to come in mean—mad as a motherfucker.

What you looking at, motherfucker?

You talkin' to a man, you motherless sombitch!

Don't fuck with me, I'll kill you!

Barking and growling—keep a stone face and a tight asshole—jump stink in a minute: they heard you was bad now you got to show 'em. What for? You slack up and they'll throw a mattress over your head. Ask some young blood from the sticks who goes upstate on some check forgery. I seen some had to have thirteen stitches in their asshole and I seen some jump off their rack with a towel wrapped around their neck 'cause some con was in love with them and they couldn't do nothin' about it—warden ain't gonna help you, hacks ain't gonna help you.

It can get nasty in there. Was a stool up there, black dude, rattin' his own people out. They caught him in the kitchen; couldn't hide the body. They cut him into little pieces, then they ground the pieces. There was a nigger in the salad that night. Nobody knowed the difference.

Then you got them little Gem blades that the guys hold in a handkerchief; don't let them corner you in the shower stall, you naked—splice you into spaghetti. That's regular, nobody say a word.

And don't be carryin' no bad habits over into the jailhouse. Had a thief stole an apple in the mess hall from the wrong guy. Guy put a wooden stake through his Adam's apple. I saw the thief spinnin' around trying to pull the stake out. He was all by himself. He didn't make it.

There's some rotten motherfuckers in there—I can take the food or the hacks, it's them criminals in there I can't stand. Like when you're short-timin', waitin' on your parole, the cons will provoke you to fight—make you blow your parole. Nasty people.

Yeah, Your Honor, check out that probation report real good—not all the kids you put in is ready for the Joint. Yeah, some of these lil' ol' boys you put in here is baby lambs and you put them in the same cage with a grizzly bear doing consecutive thirty-year bits. Rough in there, Your Honor—so like if you read the report in a hurry, read it again, 'cause you are fucking with a man's life. In America, God is dead; you the only one we got left, Your Honor—you a God. When you walk in we stand up, when you walk out we stand up. You say who lives and you say who dies—you got no boss and you can change the rules as the game goes along. So check out them lightweights good before you bury them. Now guys like me, you can deal with, 'cause I'll spit in your eye, Your Honor. I'll get to your D.A. or your cops or even to you. I may be on your hook but I'm slippin' and slidin' and one hitch and I'm gone—shit, I'll take you all on and I'll still come out on top!

I was all right in the Joint. My man Colorado was doing a deuce, and he had a little click waiting for me when I got up there. So like at chowtime Colorado is rappin' to the boys how bad I am—Carlito did this and Carlito did that. One dude, Zuzu, ain't impressed. "Aw, man, who wants to hear that shit?" Zuzu was bad, but he wasn't ready—hot soup bowl right into his face. Left hook, overhand right, then a couple kicks to the chest while he was down. Zuzu said we was only playing, but they gave me thirty days in the hole. Solder the door, motherfuckers, I don't need no bread, no water, no mail, no bed, no nothin'—Carlito is bad, ya hear, bad!

Back in population I stayed clean, worked out every day, did some reading, a lot of rapping. I seen guys go in can't read or write, come out talking Shakespeare. If you don't know nothin', the Joint is a great place—me, I had all my smarts long before.

THE WORD CAME DOWN. EARLY SIXTIES: THE GOVERNMENT was building the first big narco conspiracy cases—get them guineas, said Bobby, and they was got. Vito, Lilo, Big John, Chin, everybody went down. And the feds skinned the cats anyway they could—like with Vito— he only spoke to himself in the mirror in a Neapolitan dialect that not even an Italian could understand; mean- while, the government has him dealing with a junkie P.R. from the Bronx—who they jiving? But like they cleaned Nelson up, gave him voice lessons, a good script, and the dude came on like James Cagney. Vito got fifteen— he must have loved P.R.'s after that.

The word came down hard on Tommy Dunphy. The cons was out in the yard. Spooks, wops, P.R.'s, every- body on their own turf. I was jivin' around with the Latinos, they was bangin' on the skins as usual, timbales, conga and bongos—like a regular fuckin' band. This wal- yo type come over to me. He looked like Marc Lawrence, pinched-in, pock-marked puss. Croaky voice—some- body once told me it's because of the water in Italy, but I think it's from always talkin' in a whisper, like when you scheme. Anyway he says,

"Carlito?"

"Known by that name."

"Rocco got somethin' for ya."

We split off from my click and walk across the yard. "You're pals with Tommy Dunphy, right, Carlito?"

"Yeah, we're aces."

"He goes."

"Coño! Wait awhile—what's this?"

"Wadda you want from me, details? I don't wanna

know from nothin'. My people tell me to tell you Rocco said so-and-so. Check it out. You in or you out?"

"Okay, okay. But, Jesus, gimme a clue."

"Tommy and two other kids, brothers, handled a contract in Boston. The brothers got popped—they're giving Tommy up. The boss that ordered the hit says Tommy got to be taken out, save him the trouble of going wrong which is only a matter of time with the job busted open, *capisce*?"

"Je-sus, Tommy gotta be washed on a just-in-case."

"Wadda you want from me? I don't need this. I don't even work for Rocco or Petey A."

"All right. I'll take care of business."

"*Ciao*. 'Ey, Carlito, how can you stand that shit?"

"What choice I got? Rocco's my man."

"I don't mean that. I mean that racket from them fuckin' bongo players. Meeng!"

I was shook up—he was one of my main men, tough Irish kid from the West Side docks, good club fighter. We used to rap about being stand-up guys surrounded by rats. Bad news—I shoulda known then that I didn't fit in. But Rocco was counting on me, so I started scheming to get to Tommy—but I liked the guy, he was a down cat. So now I was sweating, kept putting the job off; some Mafioso I was gonna be. Lotta tough wops never get made 'cause they can't hurt people they ain't mad at. Ain't easy.

But got to be. Colorado had a shank he kept in a soap bar—piece of metal honed down. I caught Tommy on the ball field—caught him from behind, I didn't want to see his face—slit his throat from ear to ear; he fell on his back gagging on his own blood. I quit the scene without turning back, but I knew his eyes had to be asking Why? But he didn't go out. That night they brought a bunch of us into the hospital where he was laid out like Christ on the cross, pipes and tubes in and out of him. He was wheezing and gurgling terrible.

"Tommy, you can't make it—don't let them get away with it, you can still talk from the grave—we'll talk for you; you know you're dying—pick out the cock-sucker."

They brought us one by one to the side of the bed. He fixed his eyes on me like they was gonna pop out of his head.

"Tommy, for God's sake, just nod your head up and down—we know it's him; Tommy, you're a Christian lad—make your peace with God; don't let this bastard get away with this—give us a sign."

Tommy rolled his head—left, right, left, right. Negative. Captain Shea, there's your dyin' declaration. The rattling in his throat was getting fierce. I couldn't look at Tommy; I had tears in my eyes—fuckin' wops—my nerves were going—got to make a move.

"Shea, you Irish motherfucker, you trying to frame me."

Shea threw me a sucker right-hand which I caught on my chin—I laid down and let them carry me out. You almost had me that night, Shea, but you blew your cool.

That was a bad night—only time I ever doubted myself—what am I doing, where am I going? All that head-shrinker jive that fucks a man up—start asking questions and they got you, they into your skull. No way, Carlito;

don't let them get to your skull. You a natural-born hustler with iron balls—get the money and when they step up knock 'em down, that's all there is to it. If you start thinking and wording, then they got you, 'cause they can outthink you and outword you; then you rolling with their dice—like *society* and *humanity* and all them other *t's* that been trying to fuck you—no good. So you wronged a dude; how many times you been wronged? So he stood up—ain't he supposed to, he's a *hodedor,* ain't he? Get out my face.

In the morning I was all right. Tommy was all right, too—he recovered. Then he went back to court on some motion. They put up a big bail for him and gave him a big party.

"Tommy, there was a roundtable just before you come out and Mr. A said you done the right thing—so we're gonna move you up; you're gonna go back on the piers but with six runners turning over to you—no more unloading bananas, you stay clean. So tomorrow you run over to Leighton's, ask for Mel, tell him Mr. A sent you, get yourself five outfits—the works, look like a boss— *madon*—a donkey boss—Don Tomasino Dunferino— *uomo di onore.* Ha!"

They buried him in a lime pit. The suit had no labels but had to go for three yard easy.

Tommy, you went to your grave thinking, "That crazy Carlito tried to kill me—for no reason, spics are like that." You chump, if you had any smarts you'd have pieced it together, but they dry-humped you with a couple of quarters—you was a nickel-and-dime hustler, Tommy, but you was a good boy.

* * *

IN THE JOINT, YOU STAY UP-TO-DATE ON EVERYTHING—THINGS you wouldn't know on the street you know right away inside. Whose old lady ain't putting the horns on who. Who's teamed up with who. What crew brought in fifty keys. Who is double-crossing who. Hoodlums gossip worse than whores.

Myself, I didn't want to know if one of my old ladies was cheating on me—'cause then you got to take an attitude, then where's your packages and your visits? So I told these mothers, don't be telling me nothin' about my women. But you gonna find out anyway—like somebody's old lady be visiting and you know she's tight with your broad. "Hey, how's my old lady doing?" Real whore-like, she'll bow her head and bite her lip—"Don't ask me, man, it ain't none of my business what she's doing." Yeah, you get the message. I told all my broads when I split, "You're on your own—don't be saying how you gonna wait and all that bullshit. I ain't waiting on you!" But they still come upstate to see you; they know you're short-timing and the bread is still there—jive bitches. Lots of them drive up to the Joint with their new stud wearing your clothes and driving your car. Kiss you right on the lips too—make you a cock-sucker by proxy. Me, when I go in I don't want to know from nothin'.

SO, LIKE I PAID MY DUES TO SOCIETY AND AM READY TO take my lawful place. Shee-it, now I'm really gonna double up, deal with both hands; got to catch up, make up for that lost time—that's what drives the penologists and parole guys nuts. The criminal mind, it is a bitch. "Yes, Mr. Dunleavy, I feel that I am ready to take my lawful place in society. I realize now that I've been trying to punish my mother for making me out of wedlock."

Or like, "The man been on m'neck all m'life, but ah know now y'caint beat the man head-on with a pistol in yo' hand—you got to get yo'self a gig, make that bread, then split on out the ghetto—and thas' what I'm gonna do."

Or like, "I believe, genulmens, that if you give me parole, I'll make good this time. The therapy sessions have shown me what I got is a ethnic identity problem—yeah, ethnic identity—in other words, my people are P.R.'s—but I'm born here in the city and I resent that and there's a crisis. Then I get guilt feelings 'cause I'm putting down my own people and that's another crisis—and like that. But that's all straightened out now; I found myself and I'm ready to get that job and work hard."

Bullshit. The cons are jiving the man, but the man is jiving the cons. We know what they want to hear. And if you ain't got the mental, there's always a con to feed you your lines, somebody got a paper on it; they got habeas corpses, coram nobis, appellate division, Court of Appeals, clemency, commutation, copulation—you name it, they got a brief on it. Full of shit most of the time, but just enough to keep you hanging when they get lucky. Around '61 the Mapp case came down—all the cons went ape, everybody writing papers, and the jailhouse lawyers were ridin' high talking all that jive about searching and seizing illegal evidence. The possession cases—

dope and guns—started getting thrown out. Shit, every-body gonna get out 'cept me.

That cock-sucker Steinhardt of Four-Two-Oh Broad-way railroaded me up here. Didn't I get searched and seized? Why didn't he make a motion to suppress me? Why did Mapp have to come after me? Why wasn't it Brigante? These are the questions I wrote to him. And I reported his ass to the bar association as uncompetent counsel. And I told them how I was innocent (which I believed myself by now) and that the goddamn lawyer had defrauded me into pleading guilty. I didn't know I pleaded guilty on account of I'm a P.R. and my English ain't that good and the day of the plea I was sick with a fever plus headaches plus the lawyer guaranteed me pro-bation plus the probation report told a bunch of lies—I'll fix your Jew ass, Mr. Steinhardt.

But my writ wasn't worth a shit and they threw it out. That's me, always behind, *como los huevos del perro.* Everybody gets the word but me—everybody gets the edge but me—I got to do everything the hard way, never no break. Every favor I take I got to pay double. Uphill all the way—but I'll get even with all these mother-fuckers. I'm going out of this Joint *embalao.* I'm gonna tear up that street.

4

So I did three and change. The street, man, the street. You still hit the bricks shaky, very shaky. Like you want to see people, but you don't want to. You got it all doped out in the Joint what you gonna do the first day you're out, the second, but when you come out, you like freeze up, like you're scared but you don't know of what. So you hang 'round your crib a lot, waiting for something to happen. Didn't take long.

My man, Earl Bassey—good looking out. Took care of my bank and my crew plus his own all the time I was in. Gave me a good accounting with books and all too. Over hundred thou—I like to fall through my asshole. When you're in the Joint, anybody holds five dollars for you is a miracle. Except some of the wops—there was one boss did a long bit in a dope pinch; when he come out his crew had made and saved for him close to a million dollars in cash—so what was their reward? He's still going around checking to see if they beat him out of anything. If so, shame on them. They shoulda iced him as soon as he come out and glommed the money—they take this mafia shit too serious.

But Earl is a special kind of guy. Like they say in Spanish, *servicial*—which is ready to help anytime, down for any action. Like if you need ten large right away, Earl was there, no questions asked. If you needed good advice, Earl was the man. If you was out of coke or needed some whores in a hurry, Earl could always come up with somethin'. And how many guys can you call at 5 A.M. and tell 'em, I'm in Baldy's after-hours joint and there's three Detroit pimps here I'm gonna waste so get yo' ass down here, and he be there in a minute with two pistols, no questions asked. Earl was the best.

Lot of people thought so too. While I was in the Joint, Earl was up to being one of the main guys in Harlem. He was into everything. Even real estate in St. Croix and St. Thomas. Mr. Bassey. Earl was good with figures and books and he wanted me back in the numbers with him, but I never had no head for accounting and shit. I was just biding my time 'til I got the word from Rocco, then I was gonna invest my hundred large in a big load of junk. That's where it was at. Ain't no money nowhere else. All them hoodlums out there, hijacking trucks, robbing hotels, cracking safes, ain't shit. One connection, one move—you the man; then you can laugh up your sleeve 'cause you got the secret. So I was cool.

Meanwhile, I had me some fun. Me and a few of my boys flew down to San Juan. I paid for everything. Gambled and partied every night—had a luxury suite. Champagne breakfasts, filet mignon, hundred-dollar hookers. By this time, I was a kind of boss—I enjoyed it, about time somebody catered to me. Like if we walked into a club, my boys would flank me; I sat down first, head of the table, first choice with the broads—and the party ain't over until I say so. Whatever the topic, I was the authority; sometimes I'd cross 'em up, reverse my field, then watch the boys jerk around to get back to my new angle. Shit, I was picking up the tabs, I'm entitled. *Capo di tutti capi.* Da'sa me. Ha!

One night we ran into Llanero. Llanero was a thug from 102nd Street in Harlem, gorilla people 'cause he had a bad face with a rip on it, but inside he was a faggot and the boys would kick his ass regular. He'd go somewhere he wasn't known like the West Side or the Bronx and he'd be bad. He was a beater: Like if you didn't make a bail right away he'd be the first one on the fire escape to rob your apartment or if you had a good card game going he'd find some outside kids to stick up the joint. Me he caught with some bad candy at a party years back—"*Coño,* Carlito, this coke is special shit from the *altiplano* in Bolivia; only the chiefs snort this shit"—and an old cornet player like me like to O.D. I'd have killed the motherfucker but he was wily to find. Then he went uptown to black Harlem with a big carton of Central Park grass which he got off as Panama pot which he had sprinkled on the top. Them niggers tracked him all over the city, but when they caught up with him he talked them out of it, talking on his knees in a garbage dump in the Bronx with two pistols in his face. Llanero was tricky. We was gonna have fun with Llanero.

My man Lalin said, "Llanero, Carlito wants you to join us for dinner."

"I can't, Lalin, I got an appointment."

Loud and clear for all to hear. "Motherfucker, get yo' ass over here and sit down," says me. This was a plush restaurant in Old San Juan where the maitre d' cooks right alongside you, but I didn't give a shit.

"Sit right here at the head of the table, Llanero, you look terrific. Who you with here?"

"I'm with Santito Gil, Carlito; been here two years—clean, no problems. I heard you was doing great, Carlito; everybody in the Barrio always said, Carlito's going all the way, he's—"

"Watcha mean, motherfucker, talking behind my back—you some kind of stool pigeon? Who told you you could talk about me?"

"You got it wrong, Carlito—"

"No, you pussy, you got it wrong. I got a napkin under this table, and under that napkin there's a piece that says I'm gonna blow your stomach out your back."

Ol' scarface Llanero turned green inside his tan.

"But you look terrific, Llanero, terrific. Let's see now, them kicks you're wearing got to go for eighty dollars. Take 'em off—I mean both of them, motherfucker. That's it, cool-like. Hey, that watch, Llanero, got to be a Piaget—let Colorado hold it a minute. Let's see the label on that boss suit of yours—Louis Roth, California; I'll be damn, you must be one of them executive cats. Tato, take the jacket off him, throw it under the table. Lalin, bring the maitre d' over here."

The maitre d' had caught the action and he was all shook up.

"Waiter, what kind of ratjoint is this that a man can sit around without no jacket?"

"*Señor,* I thought he had a jacket when he came in."

"Get his ass the hell out of my table."

Llanero was in such a hurry he forgot all his gear. We slapped skin all around on the running of our little murder game.

Early that morning the Rican police hit our suite. No warrant, no nothing. Llanero to Santito to the bulls—they pull that shit over there. They give us twenty-four hours. We left standby that afternoon. I don't ever want to be busted outside of home base; that's a world of trouble.

BACK TO THE APPLE. THE JUNKIES WERE COMING OUT OF THE woodwork by now—you'd see them on rooftops, fire escapes, in alleys—hauling TV sets, toasters, radios, clothes —you name it, they was selling. Grab your coat off a wall, your hat off your head—the junkies were scavenging; get off a one high, got to get movin' to the next one; busy stealing, scheming, conning—a junkie is a busy cat, always walking fast. Watch them on 100th or 117th Street— skanky, dirty, always in pairs like faggots, never no pussy; don't want to know about no pussy, just that spike. How they got that last bag, how they gonna score the next one— that's their rap, how they're conning the world.

"Dig, Jack, I tol' Moms, you got to gimme them five dollars you got stashed, she say no good, I jumped right out on the fire escape on the edge—I'll kill myself, I don't deserve to live, I'm making you suffer, Mom. She gimme the bread. Now Wednesday when she cashes her check you wait under the stairs. I'll play chickie on the stoop, dig? But don't hurt her."

There's got to be winners and there's got to be losers. They're the losers, that's all. So when one of these chumps O.D.s, everybody's saying, what a pity, such a young man; that's what the motherfucker wants—he wants that last high, going right up the roof of his head and keep going. So what in hell is all the fuss about? They're scumbags. Get the money.

About this time Rocco Fabrizi sent for me. Jilly's. Class joint. Best piano in town. I just had Colorado with me.

"Only room at the bar, sir."

"It's okay, Mike, he's with my party."

There was five thousand years in the joint. Spitters. Rocco brought us to his table in the back—his crowd, no broads.

"You boys know Carlito, from uptown. Mr. A, I'd like you to meet Carlito."

Peter Amadeo, Rocco's boss, he's been around since they repealed Prohibition. He got three speeds—gun, knife, and the rope. Any beef or hassle come up, kill right away, then we discuss it later. He was made in the thirties, always seemed to be on the winning side in all the wars, a survivor. He come up the ladder but he ain't got no smarts, no class like Rocco. A crazy ginso with a horseshoe up his ass. Suspicious of his own mother.

"Wadda you crazy, Rocco? I got to meet people? I know too many people already—get them a table someplace else."

Real gentleman, Mr. A. I got hot but I didn't want to make more trouble for Rocco so I let it slide. Guinea motherfucker.

Rocco had them put a table for us right in the aisle. Bucket of champagne. He could see I was hot.

"The old man's very nervous, Carlito; he doesn't mean any harm, but he's got a thing about conspiracies—very nervous."

"Then maybe he ought to move over for you, Rocco."

"You're downtown now, Charles; don't fool around with that kind of talk."

"Okay, Rock, gimme the deal."

"Cubans—what do you know about Cubans?"

"The Cubans, they're here and in Miami, loads of them; what is there to know about them?"

"All right, Charles, I'll tell you. This is not a banana- or cattle-boat migration; these are doctors, lawyers, businessmen, the whole middle class—like the German Jews after the war."

"So?"

"So they're going to move fast, make their weight felt real quick-like."

"So?"

"So the hoodlums came with them. You've seen them hanging around the Latin joints down here and in Washington Heights. Light stuff feeling their way around now. But they're ex-cops and military people from the Batista and Prio governments. They're small-arms experts, they've all been in shoot-outs. They're also hungry; this is their last stop, and the pickings are easy. You get the picture now?"

"Yeah, Rocco."

"They're going to make their move. So we have to head them off at the pass, ease them in gradually. You take a few into your crew, this other guy will take some, like that. This way they won't come at us all at once. When they get greedy we'll have to kill a few but they'll be split up and all the rest will fall in line. I mean am I right or wrong?"

"You right, man, you right!"

"Things may get better because there's more than enough to go around and they're down in South America for the candy and in Europe for the real shit. I see all kinds of possibilities. Am I right or wrong?"

"The man is on, the man is on!"

"First off, you're taking a guy off my hands. They're sending him to me with his boys from Miami—yeah, your friend, Nacho Reyes; I need that crazy Cuban like a hole in the head, so I'm farming him out to you. You both eat rice and beans. Keep him under your wing, he's the main guy. If he goes along with the program, the rest will follow. Any Cubans give you trouble, send Nacho; I hear he's rough. As a matter of fact, some of my people

will be using him from time to time for various—uh—
house calls—ha!"

"*Carajo!* You gonna put this *verdugo* on me?"

"Look at that, you even talk the same language. Tell
your man to get you your car, I'll walk you to the corner."

When we got to Eighth Avenue, Rocco said, "There's
a car on its way over now—I'm forming a pot, ten guys,
a hundred a piece."

"You running the deal?"

"Who else?"

"I'm in."

"Take this half of a dollar bill; Vinnie—you remember Vinnie—he'll have the other half on him; he'll be at
your place Tuesday, have fifty ready for him—front
money. Have the rest ready for Friday—C.O.D., I'm
guaranteeing the shit."

"Rocco, you know what this means to me, I'll never
let you down."

"I told you I'd give you a shot; it's a welcome-home
present from your Uncle Cheech—'ey *afangul,* wadda
you gonna kiss me on the cheek? Get uptown."

And the deal went down. Ten kilos I got. We had that
shit in the street in no time. I was big-time. Imagine, me,
Carlito, the main connection uptown. I knew I was bad,
but I didn't know I was slick.

About this time I changed my image—conservative
clothes, a pad on the East Side, a Lincoln. I even bought
a discotheque downtown so I could get next to the young
pussy that was down there—the help was robbing me but
I didn't give a shit, it was just a toy. Funny the way the

wise-guy can never make it in legit business because
the square that covers for him will always rob him.
Never fails. I guess it's like getting even. I used to like
to stash into the joint with a big party. Champagne for
everybody—make believe I was checking the receipts.
"I don't want nobody in my joint with a piece"—law and
order—when I think of the bread I've pissed away!
Sometimes on a Saturday I'd jump up to Harlem in my
Lincoln and play stickball in the street with the kids in
my eighty-five-dollar slacks. Yeah, I was a big shot!
Everybody said it, *"Carlito buena gente!"* Like if some
P.R.'s was getting dispossessed or needed some funeral
money, I'd see them go. Or if some dude come out of
the slams or couldn't make a bail, I was always down.
Like I wouldn't hog the bread—everybody with me went
first-class. Especially my broads—you name it, good
clothes, good jewelry, good coke.

   Then the Cubans punched in. *Cubiches!* They sure
shook up the hoodlums. Right away they was ringside
at all the Latin joints drinking Chivas Regal and snorting. They call coke *perico* (parakeet) because it makes
you talk all night. So they'd be in the after-hours joints
until 10 or 11 A.M. Everybody had a pistol so it was Wild
West stuff. A pistola they call a *fuca*—so when you mix
perico and *fucas* you know you got trouble. People were
getting killed. Ask the bulls from the two-eight, the three-
oh, and the three-four—they thought a hurricane had hit
Manhattan. The hoodlums were all shook up, everybody
was packing; mostly the Cubans would fight among
themselves but it was only a question of time.

Nacho Reyes: first night in New York we hit about ten joints—Liborio, Iberia, La Baracca, like that. He had put a group together in Miami, all hitters, all veterans of the Batista wars, all hungry. The Ricans quite naturally had to be the hosts.

Nacho's tongue was always thick from *perico,* which he snorted day and night, so when you talked he always got up close to your face—*"Mi hermano, mi consorte."* If he wanted to get somethin' across to you he'd close his eyes in the middle of a sentence and leave his mouth open—so you'd be waiting. Before you knew it I was doing the same thing. *"Mi her-mano,"* crazy. His life was unreal. He'd killed four cops, two of Batista's and two of Castro's. His mortal enemy, Juanito Cuatro Vientos (Johnny Four Winds), had shot him five times in an ambush in Havana. They took him to the morgue where he came to on a slab. He got up off the slab naked with the five bulletholes and stumbled into the morgue attendant's office—scared the shit out of the guy.

When Nacho was a prisoner in Isla de Pinos, the Castro militia would take him to *paredón* each dawn, and the firing squad would shoot blanks at him. Bad for your nerves. He killed two Castro cops, stole a jeep, and sneaked into the Mexican embassy dressed like a Western Union guy. In Mexico, he was working for the C.I.A. shooting Castro agents. Yeah, baby, we play rough, too. Nacho's boys was no slouches, either. They all been trained with the Rangers in the U.S. Army, in Florida and Guatemala, had jumped off at the Bay of Pigs and the Belgian Congo.

Nacho himself was not a hustler—he didn't racketeer. His business was his balls. In other words, if he heard that Rolando from Union City had made a score, he would drop in on him and hit him for five hundred or so. Or if maybe Mario from Miami was in town with a big bundle, Nacho would get next to him. No gorilla or stick-up shit, more like, "*Mi hermano,* I am short on funds to continue my fight against Castro and Communism; I know you want to give your share." Guys like Rolando and Mario were bad-asses and they really weren't afraid of Nacho, it's just that Nacho was like supported by all the Cuban wise-guys; so even though they weren't scared of him, they weren't ready to die any day of the week the way he was, and besides, if they had a problem of violence they could count on Nacho any time of the day or night no matter who or what was involved. It could be a beat—*tumbe*—for twenty thou or a piece of ass, all the same to Nacho.

Right away, he was trouble for me. That first night, we hit an after-hours place in the East Sixties. Connected people own the joint. Hoodlums and whores all crowded together carrying on even though straight people are already getting up to go to work. Nacho says to his boys, "Manolito Matanzas!" Oops! *Qué pasa* with Manolito Matanzas? I see this tall skinny guy all dressed in white, in winter. "He is making his *santo,* I see; then this is a good time to blow him to hell."

"Wait a minute, Nacho, what's wrong with this guy?"

"He is an *hijo de puta* from Matanzas who was one of the jailers at Isla de Pinos. I told him that whenever I saw him, he would be mine. Tonight I keep my promise."

"Nacho, the people here are friends of mine, *Italianos;* we got to show respect."

"Fuck the *Italianos,* Manolito's time has come. But we will give him a fair chance. Camaguey, give me your pistol; take the bullets out of the clip."

Camaguey took the bullets out of the clip, then slid the empty magazine back into the automatic and handed the gun to Nacho.

Nacho yelled from the bar to Manolito's table, "Manolito Mantanzas, you are a *maricon* and a *hijo de puta-echa pa'lante si eres hombre.*"

The joint wasn't jumping anymore. Stand back. Matanzas was glue—he kept his hands on top of the table, but he wouldn't look up.

"Nacho Reyes, I do not have a gun on me, I am making my *santo* and I do not want any trouble."

"You made plenty trouble in Isla de Pinos when you had your gun and stick. You were an *abusador* but I told you then your time would come. Look at my face, *cabron!*"

"I do not have a gun."

"Then I will give you a gun, *maricon!*" And Nacho pulled out Camaguey's automatic and placed it out on Matanzas' table, all the time holding his own revolver in his right hand.

"*Agarra,* Manolito, *agarra!*"

"No, Nacho, I will not fight you with this gun. Give me the one in your hand; that's the one I want, you take this one."

Manolito was no fool.

With that, Nacho busted Matanzas across the face and head with the pistol butt until the blood ran all over the white suit. All hell broke loose now, chairs flying, women screaming. We quit the joint in a hurry. We drove down to another after-hours in the East Twenties. We weren't there long when I got to feeling sick from all the shit I'd put in my nose—out of training, I guess. Nacho walked me outside to the street. All of a sudden, I see Manolito Matanzas running behind the parked cars across the street; he's got a carbine with a banana clip.

"Duck, Nacho!"

Pow, pow, pow—we're running but the carbine is plowing up the asphalt all around us—Nacho hits the ground, spins around, and empties his piece at Matanzas. By this time, Nacho's boys are down and shooting. Matanzas is down. "Look what you've done to me!" Last words. Later for Matanzas. Dump all the guns and let's get out of here.

Nacho was hit in the sole of his foot, blowing out the bones in his instep. Don't ask me how, but right there in his dingy hotel room, a Cuban doctor put wires in Nacho's foot, sewed him up, put a cast on the leg. Nacho stayed in the room a week, snorting coke. After a week he was getting around on crutches, no infection, no nothing. That cocaine will cure anything. Anybody else they would have had to cut the leg off at the thigh. Sombitch is indestructible. There was a roundtable about the brawl inside the East Sixties spot but Rocco straightened it out.

The Cubans were all *santeros*. They believe in the saints. Saint Lazarus, Santa Barbara, like that. I been to Cuban homes where they'll have a special room for the saint. A plaster saint maybe five feet tall with a golden sword with real jewels in it and a velvet cape and a golden crown. Then they put food around the saint. They are sold on this stuff, can't tell them different. Then they got all kinds of hexes and voodoo. With big money being paid to the *santera* or *santero*. Like if a Cuban wants something real bad he promises to do his *santo* if he gets it. His *santo* might be giving up several thousand dollars, shaving his head bald, dressing only in white.

The Ricans got their hocus-pocus too—*espiritistas,* we call them. If they done a *trabajo* (a job) on you, you're in trouble, you're hexed—everything gets fucked up. The Latin hoodlums believe all that shit, so if they got a big deal cooking they get a job done, or if they been getting busted too often they get a job done to get the hex off them. I seen stone racketeers and killers going in for this shit. Me, I don't believe in nothin' but that dollar bill in my pocket—stay with the money, you be all right. You can be broke in China or Cuba where everybody is in the ditch, but how you gonna be broke and in the ditch here when you got them guys driving by you with Cadillacs splashing mud in your face? No way. Throw it all up in the air and see who comes up with what—I'll take my chances.

The Cubans were roaming around, looking for a soft spot. The cops were expecting an all-out war, but it never come off because there was more than enough to go around. Except for a few cowboys like Rocco, the wops were afraid of the junk, and the Ricans and the Blacks never got connected overseas. But junk was king. So the Cubans filled the gap—with no money, no connections, no language, they set up on the East Coast, West Coast, Europe, South America. Unbelievable. They got heavy in no time. They had respect for the old pros like me, but once in a while they'd show their teeth.

Like there was this guy Rivas-Barcelo. He'd been a big shot in Cuba, minister of transportation under Prio; he sold the whole transportation stock in Havana and pocketed the money. Then when Batista came in, he was a boss in the secret police under Ventura. He'd walk into a precinct where they had some Castro suspects—"How come these men are still alive?" They wouldn't stay alive long. Stone killer but he always wore dark suits with vests and a homburg hat—with his gray hair, he looked like a judge. I liked to rap with him. He always spoke with a Castilian accent, and even if they was raunchy whores, he'd be bowing and pulling out chairs, "*señorita*" this and "*señorita*" that. He wore shades day and night but it didn't do any good, you could still see his eyes; you knew he would never hesitate. He brought his boys out of Cuba with him on one of the last boats to get out. Rivas paid the skipper in counterfeit money, but the skipper had the last laugh because he didn't know where he was going and they got lost all over the Gulf of Mexico. A couple of Rivas' boys couldn't cut it and had to be dumped to the sharks. The rest made it on account of Rivas kept them going when they about had it. They called him *Comandante*.

Rivas had some tough boys but one in particular, Roberto Palacios, was a very nasty kid, psycho-like. Palacios was around twenty-one years old but had been shooting people in Havana, Miami, and New York. He'd come into the joints and walk from one end of the bar to the other bad-eyeing everybody; then he'd go outside and come back to find out if somebody was saying something about him. He kept all the thugs on edge because you knew somebody had to kill him and you wondered if you was gonna be the lucky guy to lock with him. Rivas used to say he was a *buen muchacho* from a wealthy family who had lost everything. Then Rivas decided to aim the kid at us. One night I was at a joint near Amsterdam Avenue with my group and Rivas and his *bravos* had a table nearby. All of a sudden Palacios says to my man Victor Lopez, "You're sitting in my chair."

Victor don't take no shit nohow—"Fuck, you mean I got your chair?"

"You are lacking in respect for me, Victor."

"Wadda you crazy, man? Get out of here before I knock you on your ass."

"I am going to my car, meet me outside in ten minutes, bring something with you."

Palacios left. Rivas did not say a word to Palacios, instead he ordered a round of drinks for my table. "This is not our affair, Carlito, let these impetuous youngsters settle their differences; if we all go outside there might be a tragedy—Victor's blood is hot, let him go out."

So that's how it went down—one on one. When we got outside, Palacios was dead and Victor had three bullets in him. We got rid of both pistols before the Man came. I got to Victor first—"Not a word to the bulls, name and address, that's all—don't talk about no self-defense, don't say nothin', on advice of counsel!" They kept Victor at the Bellevue Prison Ward. I told his old lady, "You tell Victor that I am conducting his defense, he don't need no goddamn lawyers; the grand jury got to know that Victor acted in self-defense, and where is the piece for the possession charge? No case, the man got to walk."

The grand jury dismissed the case. Everybody uptown was saying how Carlito knew the law better than the lawyers. Goddamn right. After that I was giving out all kinds of legal decisions in all the joints. I missed my calling, shoulda been a judge. Will the party of the first part sit down so I can talk to that fine party of the second part in my chambers? Or like I charge this jury that that cop is a lying sombitch and you better come in with a verdict of acquittal 'cause I'm going to dismiss the case anyhow. Or I hereby order the D.A. committed for ninety days for contempt of court for presenting such a shit-ass case. And I hereby order the stool pigeon to the Elmira Reception Center for an indeterminate sentence and suspend sentence on the defendant. History-making decisions.

The Cubans livened things up and we had a lot of fun with them. Nobody can party like them.

5

I HAD PLENTY OF BUCKS BUT ONLY FROM THE JUNK—everything else I did lost money. And I was always angling for schemes—like this middleweight who's knocking 'em dead in the gym. When I'm promoting, every time he steps in the ring he gets knocked on his ass. Then there was this chanteuse who was gonna be another Olga Guillot, cost me a bundle—had to get her an apartment and everything. She couldn't sing worth a damn; we'd spring her on the Cubans in Union City and Hoboken with a big promotion—no dice. Seem like dealing is all I'm good at, so be it.

Earl Bassey was married by now and he'd tell me, "You got to get yo'self a good old lady and settle down. Look at me, I got me a home on the Island, a wife and a kid. Come Sunday I lay up like a respectable citizen. I'm putting it all together and in a little while my lil' brother Reginald is gonna have the whole thing and I'm retiring to St. Croix. I got me the bread, what for I'm gonna wait 'til the Man puts me back in striped pajamas? No good.

You know I ain't ever jived you, Carlos, I'm telling you in front—the party's over. The Man be cooking up the conspiracies again, but the sentences are gonna be a motherfucker—I ain't jiving you, I got this from some big people. Get yo' ass out now, bro, 'cause in a little while it gonna belong to the government. That's the sermon for today."

"You right, Earl, I been thinking the same thing." Bullshit. I always agree with what people tell me and it sounds good at the time, but then I go my way anyway. But I didn't go for the bit about his kid brother Reggie. Now that was a bad nigger. Earl brought him up out of Philly where he was going to college. Earl had a blind spot for the kid. Reggie would strut around uptown with these two flunkies of his, dressed in some Fidel Castro overalls. Everything was "black" this and "black" that. When he first come up to New York, I was at the Baby Grand with some tan chick and he wanted to know what my white face was doing in the joint. Meanwhile, I knew he had a white bitch in the Village. The shit was straightened out but I knew he was trouble.

About this time I got hung on a broad bad. Her name was Leticia but I called her Tuta, like a nickname I give her. She reminded me of India in looks but she wasn't no *bollo-loco* like India, she was a clean girl. As a fact she was the first "good" girl I ever had. She was a very educated girl, been to high school and everything. I met her downtown in a joint I was eating at with my buddy. We noticed these two dolls at this table next to ours. So right away I sent them over a drink—no good, not interested. Then, like to made to order, some guy stoned comes over to their table and starts breaking chops. Right away, I jump up and grab the guy by the arm and pull him away.

I say, "Can I talk to you a minute, sir? I'm Detective Russo of the vice squad and I couldn't help but notice you were disturbing these young ladies. Now run along before you get yourself in trouble."

"Where'sh your identification?"

"After I show you my shield, I'm going to kick your ass through that plate-glass window."

He split. "Ladies, I'm sorry about this man disturbing you, I don't think he'll bother you anymore."

A while later, the waiter come over and said the ladies would accept our drink. Well all right!

She fell out when she saw my white Lincoln what I was rolling around in at the time. She didn't want me to drive her home but I insisted—then I found out why; she lived in the projects off 106th Street and Madison Avenue, a rose in spic Harlem. Them projects been low in income but high on beautiful girls. I got to hanging around the Gondolier and Sunlite bars on Madison and 104th to be near her. We snuck around a lot, I didn't want everybody to know I was going serious with a young thing. She was only nineteen. Like all Latin chicks, she loved to dance. She had me dancing at the Chateau Madrid, Corso's, the Ginza. I'd take her to the Garden to fights. I'd pick her up at her office and we'd go to dinner, like Forno's for Spanish or Sal Anthony's for Italian. Without realizing it, I got involved with the broad.

It got so we had to see each other every day, and I wasn't even screwing her. I was worried about it, what the hell's going on here? Like, I wasn't myself; I don't talk on the phone for nobody—but her, we'd talk for hours. I wasn't snorting or even carrying a piece. Then I was thinking maybe I'm going to get married. Jesus. One day she talked me into meeting her family. Mistake. Her folks were all right—I came on with mucho *señora* and *señor.* But Tuta's older brother Sigfrido was there. And he wasn't buying no tickets off'n me. He looked at me like I was the devil himself. He had a grocery down the block and he knew my story from A to Z. This was a square who worked behind a counter sixteen hours a day—you know he was gonna love my ass. After he got through choking he called a family conference—I heard words like *delincuente, maton, droguero*—I eased out of the apartment. And even feeling relieved. This ain't my bag. But a few days later, Tuta got to me; she was crying and saying that she wanted to give me a chance to explain. I told her, "I have been in trouble before but that's because I was an orphan; I didn't have no family to look out for me like you, so I was always getting blamed for everything because I had no one to stick up for me. On account of my record I can't get a decent job, God knows I tried everything. So I turned to gambling and made a few dollars which I have invested in a bar—I lied to you when I told you I was in real estate because I knew you'd put me down for my past record. That's where it's at, Tuta. I've leveled with you—now you can believe in me or

believe the goddamn lies and rumors these jealous Puerto
Ricans are gonna tell you."

It was one of the best speeches I ever gave a broad and
she dug it. Meanwhile, she was eating sirloin steaks and
drinking champagne and sitting ringside—that helped.
She came my way. Now we really had to sneak around.

Came a long weekend and Tuta told her family she was
going with her girlfriends to the Spanish villas around
Newburgh. We flew to Miami. *Qué* party! La Guillot,
Manzanero were singing down there. Los Violines,
Montmartre—the whole Cuban scene. Yeah, mother, I
got to them drawers. Got my head bad too. I was really
hung up on her. She knew she had me staggering behind
her box. She demanded that we elope. I was groggy but
not that groggy. I retaliated with, "I was married many
years ago, as a minor, but I'm working on my divorce
now. Then we'll get married right away." Ain't no rug
can lie better than me.

It was fab'lous honeymoon without benefit of clergy.
But now it was time to pay my dues. We arrived Tuesday night looking tanned 'n terrific. I drove her up to
104th Street to let her cross the street by herself. I waited
on the corner until she was out of sight, then I decided to
go into the Gondolier for a taste. Sigfrido came in from
my right. I had no piece—the first one hit me flush on
the chest; I tried to grab him, but he put two more in my
stomach. The guys from the Gondolier came running out.
"Carlito's dead," "They killed Carlito," people yelling.
And I was going out. I was freezing, maybe I'm dead

already. I couldn't see, but I could hear voices. I wanted
to get up but couldn't move. I remembered other guys
dying on the streets of Harlem wanting to get up as if you
couldn't die standing up. The bulls—"Wait for an ambulance," "Some dope pusher named Carlito, I know
him," "Sure punched his ticket."

Then Cheo from the Gondolier said, "Don't wait for
no fucking ambulance—don't leave him there—what
about my fucking license? Carry him to the Flower Hospital—it's only a block away." Cheo saved my ass.

I was dying for two weeks, especially around early dawn
I'd really fade, but I kept coming back. Them doctors like
to croak me, but I survived just for spite. Like the bullet
in my chest, they couldn't find it. It's still in there—I don't
bother him, he don't bother me. In the evening, everybody
would come in to see me, everybody but Tuta. They told
me she and her whole family had checked out that same
night. Figured I'd have the brother killed. No way. You
know that chump had to be sore, peddling *bacalao* and
plátanos in a store the size of a closet. And me with my
pimp-car running off with his sister. Shit, he was smoking. Me, I ain't no grudgeholder—if I had caught the dude
early on, I'd a put a hurtin' on him, but later on—what the
hell? Fact is, Sigfrido did me a favor—I felt better every
day, like I took a weight off. Always felt that way when I
shook off a broad—don't have to account to nobody—stay
loose—if I'm busted don't have to worry she's cheating
on you. My line of work, man only supposed to worry
about one thing: staying out the Joint. Anything else is
superfluid.

The bulls from the two-three was up to see me regular. First time I was a complainant.

"They was three muggers, hofficer. Mean, too. Didn't give me a chance to hand over my money. A man cannot walk in the streets 'cause Lindsay has tied your hands—a regular ghetto here in the two-three, I'm moving up to Simpson Street where a man is safe."

"You always been a wise cock-sucker, Carlito—that's why they perforated your ass. Listen, if it was up to me they coulda buried you, but we got these reports and we gotta have a description of the assailants—now quit fucking around!"

"Well, your honor, the assailants looked colored, but they might have been dark Italians or even that other group you got around here. In the dark, *todos los gatos son negros.* Don't get mad at me, officer, all I saw was bang, bang, bang. I wouldn't want to make no mistake, I know what it is to be framed by your house."

"Aw, you wise—!"

"Don't mess with Hoppy, pres, I'm a sick man." Man, would I break their hole!

Last time I heard, Tuta got married down in P.R. I dug her, I can't deny it, but my way is still best. Loose. But *un clavo saca otro,* and pretty soon I was cruising around with this bandit from Brooklyn. Uweee, you devil. I got back into the groove real quick-like. They was robbing me in my disco joint but I was getting plenty of pussy out of there.

The horse was riding high. But getting harder to come by. What with the government and the stool pigeons a lot of heavyweights was getting put away. The heat was on something fierce. But all the better for the guys that really knew what's happening. That's money, baby, money. Be a fool to walk away from that. Myself, I'm down for the action anytime, and I don't want to hear this ol' bullshit about the little kids in the schoolyard. The only ones dealing with the little kids is the little kids themselves, and if people want to get high, that's their lookout. Shit, if they ain't on junk, they'll be on wine or some other shit. They can't cope—shame on them. I'm short-timing in this world and any way I get by is okay with me. I only know one way—my way, like the song. Frank'll tell you.

About that time, Rocco had a baptismal affair for his new baby boy at his house out on the north shore. Me and Earl drove over to pay our respects. Reggie came too—seem like Rocco told Earl to bring his kid brother, Reggie, along. With Earl pulling out I guess Rocco wants to make sure Reggie can step in without no hitch. It was an afternoon affair on Rocco's big lawn, catered, very nice. There was some heavy people there, including Rocco's uncle, Dominick Cocozza. Cocozza ranked Amadeo, so for the first time I seen Amadeo not acting like an animal. Cocozza would talk and Amadeo would "Yeah, Dom" and "Right, Dom." Amadeo told Cocozza what a great guy Rocco was and what a great money-maker he was for the outfit. He also said he had his son Paul moved in two houses down so that some of Rocco's smarts could rub off on Paul. Everybody was drinking and feeling pretty good. Cocozza told Earl, "My nephew's told me what a great help you been to him uptown, that your word is good. A man's word must be sacred. Not like these punks and stool pigeons coming up. *Combinazione,* that's the ticket, we work together; you make money, we make money. Let's drink to that." Everybody was drinking except Amadeo and Reggie.

Rocco pulled me over to a corner. "You remember Sixto Davila?"

"Yeah, Rock, quarter-key man from the Bronx, up in Prospect. He was at the El when we was there."

"Right. While you were away we tried to help him—he was always crying, gimme a break, Rocco, so I gave him a break—a heavy number. He dealt the goodies, but being a garbage can he showed his hand on the first deal—glommed the money and he took off to Europe. I didn't say anything because Petey A gets excited and I made up the money. Now I don't believe in hurting a guy over money, most of the time you're getting off cheap. But I have a man in Madrid and this Sixto has gotten to him and he's giving my man a big play. I say Sixto is a beater and a beater is the next thing to a rat. I say he's stooling for Interpol."

"Which does what for me?"

"You're going to Spain, Carlito!"

"I ain't no hit man, Rocco, why not Nacho?"

"A Cuban has trouble getting in and out; and besides, this is not a cowboy job. You get next to him, get his guard down; the hit will come from somewhere else. This is important, Charles."

"Whatever you say, Rocco."

"Vinnie will be around to see you tomorrow with the details."

Almost didn't make that trip. Got pinched—me and this guy, Chángui—and while I was on a mission for mercy, mind you. My ol' buddy Lino, the barber, was dyin' in the Mount Sinai—doctors said he was terminal. I used to see him regular, he didn't want for nothin'. Lino had looked out for me when I was a kid. Anyway, he asks me for a favor. Seem his son, Felino Jr., known as Junior (no fuckin' good), was doin' a lot of scratchin' and eatin' a lot of jelly rolls. Lino was suspectin' he was on junk. Now I follow the golden rule about mindin' m'own business, but what the hell—I owed Lino. So me and this guy Chángui go lookin' for Junior. We find out that he was scorin' out of a Bickford's on 145th Street and Broadway. He didn't wanna come out the joint, so we dragged him outside, put him against a building, and give him a few smacks. Then we tried to reason with him. I told him if his father was a barber without no schoolin' he could be a doctor if he had some schoolin'; he said he was in a trade school, Machine and Metal Trades on 96th Street. Wise cock-sucker. Then be a fuckin' dentist, and I gave him another rap. I read him the riot law—if I find out you're using hard shit I'm gonna pull your tongue out yo'ass, etc.

About this time, four detectives come out of an unmarked car with their cannons out. *Puñeta.* Me and Chángui get tossed up against the wall. They chased Junior. They got our pistols and they got eight yard I had in my pocket. This is after 4 A.M., 'cause the crowd from the Caborojeño Club upstairs had already let out. The bulls take me and Chángui down to Riverside Park. Ain't no precinct in there, so I know we gonna settle out of court. Moldy-puss was the main bull of the four, he said,

"Watcha names, punks?"

"I'm Inspector Moran, this is Lieutenant Chángui."

"I'll bust your ass, Brigante. I know you—what the hell are you doin' this far up in a cheap shakedown?"

"We were just tryin' to straighten the kid out for his father."

"Oh, I see, juvenile aid work, eh? Your ass. We gotcha for assault and possession of loaded guns. How do you like them onions?"

"The kid won't sign no complaint, and this was an illegal search—we weren't committin' no crime. Bust won't stick."

"You fuckin' hump—we went to question you, you stumbled, fell against me. I felt the bulge on your hip. Gotcha. Right, guys?"

I know when I'm in an over-the-weight match.

"Officer, that eight hundred ain't mine. S'pose we split down the middle. That'll give you guys a hundred a piece, right? Everybody wins."

"Wrong. You are a cheap cock-sucker, Brigante; you're lucky you're dealin' with me. Beat it."

They kept the guns too. Mother-hoppers. I got back to Lino next day and told him what he wanted to hear, that the kid was only sniffin', not skin-poppin', and that he was straightened out. The kid was straight like a fishhook. Can't do nothin' with a *tecato*. Lalin's kid brother, Narciso—forty-dollar-a-day habit—jab himself in the cock and in the neck. Once, Lalin knocked his teeth out—didn't do no good. From the whole army of junkies marchin' around Harlem I ain't seen but two guys walk away from the spike.

It didn't matter Lino none—them doctors finally terminaled him. *Adiós, buena gente, descanse en paz.*

I would have gone for the funeral, but he had insurance. I put some bread on Lino's widow, Doña Mercedes. It didn't take Junior long to put Doña Mercedes in the box next to Lino. I cried at that funeral; she was a lady.

Don't look at me. I never put no needle in nobody's arm. How many Juniors have I tried to straighten out? Shit, I'm just gettin' by myself. Plenty bites been taken outa my ass—lucky I got a rhino hide and a concrete skull. Else my ass would be grass now too.

6

$V_{\textit{IVA ESPAÑA}}$! MADRID, A CLASS TOWN. RIGHT AWAY I
liked it. Clean, big boulevards. Everybody's a square, no
angling. Almost everybody; Don Jorge Betancourt,
Rocco's man, came by my hotel the first night I was in
town. An older guy, European-type cat—like a head-
waiter, very dignified, with a heavy theta sound I had to
get used to. I never heard that kind of Spanish in the
Barrio. But we got to rapping pretty good. I told him this
had to be wham-bam-thank you Ma'm because I had to
get back to New York. We put on a terrific feed that night,
then we went bouncing around the *tablaos*. Fantastic-
looking heads—Gypsies. This might be fun. Second joint
we hit we run into Sixto. The joint was shaped like a cave,
with a lot of Gypsies singing and dancing. Don Jorge
spotted him first—"He is here, on the left near the stage;
his man is with him." Sure enough, there was Sixto
Davila yelling "*Olé tu madre*" with the best of them like
a regular *Gallego*—jive Puerto Rican. We were cool,
didn't look his way. Sure enough, a bucket of champagne

arrived, compliments of *el señor* in the corner. He come over. I threw my arms around him. "Sixto, my man! You look terrific, put on some good weight. The hell you doing in Spain, I thought you was in the Joint?"

"I been moving around a lot, Carlito. I got bored of New York and P.R. Figure I'd check the scene over here."

Jorge said, "So you know Carlito well, Sixto? Well, Carlito, you are now better recommended. I have much affection for Sixto, a man of *condiciones* and respect—perhaps we can be friends."

I picked it up. "Don Jorge, Sixto will tell you that I am a man of honor and when I give my word that is my life—*no es así,* Sixto?"

"The man don't lie, Don Jorge; you can count on Carlito Brigante, anytime—I back him up hundred per cent."

You stool-pigeon motherfucker.

Don Jorge went to rap with some people there so I leaned over to Sixto—"*Mi hermano,* I won't forget this—you don't know what this means to me. I need this connection bad; a guy in the Joint put me on to Don Jorge—he got to give me a break, this may be my last chance to make it after all those years I suffered in the can."

I put on like my crying face, like uptight. Sixto bit good—"Don't worry, Carlito, the old dude is in my pocket; he will deal with you—what the hell are friends for? After all the shit we been through together! How long since you been out on the street?"

"Just a few days, ain't had a chance to see nobody. Wanted to hook up with this man right away. I want nothing to do with them motherfuckers from before; they all let me down when I was in the Joint—fuck 'em."

"That's what I say, Carlito—fuck 'em where they breathe."

Well all right. So me and Sixto got tight—had to be, he was lonely for New York. So we partied for days, me not acting too flush so Sixto was thinking I was hungry for bread. After a couple of days we sprung the trap.

"Look, Sixto, while the old man is in the john, let me level with you fast. I ain't got no bread, I'm here to rip off this Jorge faggot. I got a line on some big bucks he got stashed away plus a meet he's got on the border this weekend for two hundred keys. Sixto, this is the maximum shot we ever gonna have. I need your help, Sixto."

"*Coño,* Carlito, *coño!*"

"We can't talk here, this old motherfucker has spies all over Madrid. Tomorrow I'm driving out to Franco's tomb, El Valle de los Caidos, near Segovia."

"I know where it is."

"I'll meet you there at 3 P.M. and we can scheme in private. Cool it, here he comes. 3 P.M.—come alone and make sure you're not tailed."

That morning, Vinnie and his man Lucien showed up at my room. Lucien was a demolitions guy from North Africa, knew his stuff.

"Okay, Vinnie, I'll follow your car out to the tomb. We'll both park in the lot by 2 P.M. Make sure we're there first—he'll show early to check out the scene, he's a suspicious and jumpy sombitch. I'll go out and put my arm around him—I'll take him up to the top of the cross. Slap

the bomb on his car but give it a half hour. After I'm upstairs fifteen minutes you and Lucien come up—he'll get
suspicious right away, think it's a setup—he'll run. Give
him five minutes to get down to his car; ten minutes he's
driving down the mountain—boom. Later for Sixto. Got
the picture, Vin?"

"Uhuh."

"Some pair you are; Lucien can't talk English and you
are a goddamn mute."

"What's to talk, Carlito? We know the way out there
and we got the firecracker—you just point him out. One
thing—what makes you so sure he'll run when he sees
me and Lucien?"

"You kidding? One look at your guinea puss and this
fuckin' A-rab of yours and he'll bolt like a rabbit—I
know my man."

Next day, we drove out on schedule. Not ten minutes
after we pulled into the parking area Sixto arrived. A
beater is always on time. If a guy is right he don't rush
because he's sure, but a schemer can't afford no delay,
so he's always on time. You don't read these things in
no book, you just got to develop the vibes. Trouble is too
many guys get wasted before they hip up. Shame on
them.

It was a cold fall day, sun was shining. No one around
hardly. "Sixto, my man, you're early, I like that—I can't
stand these cats that ain't never on time. Let's go to the
top together." We took the elevator up, just me and Sixto.
The elevator shaft cuts right through the heart of the
mountain, clear up to the peak. There they built like a

giant platform, and on top of this a stone cross 450 feet high. They've cut men riding on animals out of stone at each of the four corners of the platform. But each figure maybe sixty feet high. Cannot be believed what Spanish sweat has worked here. Forget about the Pyramids, the Valley of the Fallen is the maximum. A hell of a monument to Spanish blood. I wonder if it covers the Spanish blood spilling in the hallways and alleys of Harlem, if it got room for the Latins O.D.ing on the rooftops of the South Bronx. Something happened to my people since they come across the water.

It's cold on top of that mountain and the wind blows strong. If you look straight up at the cross with the clouds blowing over it, you get dizzy, like the cross is swaying and gonna fall on top of you. Not to be believed.

"There's no one around, Carlito."

"Oh, yeah, Sixto. I wanted to get together with you on this business I told you about last night, but early this morning some people got to me with a bad report about you—now I ain't saying I believe it, Sixto. You know me, I always like to give a man a chance to explain."

"Is this from the wops, Carlito?"

"Yeah, like you beat them—"

"That money was coming to me, they was humping me on the deal—you'd have done the same thing."

"Including me being a rat, Sixto?"

His eyes popped, so I knew he'd seen Vinnie and Lucien. He was gone. We waited awhile. Everything was real quiet, just the wind blowing up there like on the roof of the world. Boom. Later for Sixto.

Before I left, Don Jorge came to me with, "Carlito, I have been much impressed with your *hombría;* perhaps we can work together directly. I mean, we are Latinos, why need you work behind these people?" Right away, I knew Mr. Petey Amadeo was in the junk business. I recognized Amadeo's handwriting right away. Check. Double-check. Triple-check. Cross. Double-cross. Triple-cross. I knew Don Jorge was in bed with Amadeo. And the *cornuto* is Rocco. Amadeo's got Rocco taking all the weight what goes with being a dope pusher—meanwhile he's clean to all including Rocco. All the time Don Jorge got to report to Amadeo.

"No, *mil gracias,* Don Jorge, but I could never go it alone and I am grateful that they should give me this chance."

"Your loyalty is touching, I commend you for it. *Adiós.*"

So Amadeo is looking for an excuse to have me washed. And first dollar Rocco steals, Don Jorge will rat him out and Amadeo will have him. Amadeo can't cook up deals to make money like Rocco and he ain't read no books, but he is a crafty motherfucker. That's why he been attending other people's funerals since the thirties. These fuckin' wops, they ain't satisfied with loading the dice, they got to stick you up after the game too. I'm over my head. I'm getting out; I'm gonna tell Rocco as soon as I get back.

7

I GOT BACK TO NEW YORK. BUT I DIDN'T SAY NOTHIN' TO Rocco about Don Jorge and Amadeo. In the life, a man cannot be involved with words, like who said what about who—for sure you'll be in the middle. In other words, you can rat out a ratter but you can't rat out a double-crosser. Some fuckin' business. I started partying like crazy again. Rivas *el Comandante* had run into a crew of teenage boldykes, so we was renting hotel suites, feeding the dykes coke, and watching the show. That Rivas was a stone degenerate but he sure could dig up some freaky broads.

About this time Reggie started hanging out with me. Earl told me, "I want my bro out them goddamn dungarees—I tol' him, how you gonna command respect? Lookin' like a reject from the janitor's union. I tol' him he got to move around, not just in Harlem, get to deal all around, we're black and proud of it but that don't mean we got to beat our chest all the time, it ain't cool, and it sound like you don't believe it yo'self. I tol' him that I am leaving for good and if he want to be the main man he got to clean himself up—and iffen he don't, then I'm just gonna pass him up for somebody—like Carlito."

"Thanks a million, Earl, you got some sense of humor."

"I don't get out much anymore, Carlito, I been busy getting everythin' together—you on the street all the time, take Reginald under your wing once in a while, show him the Latin action, like that. If he gonna be a boss he got to get rounded out, y'dig?"

"I dig."

Reggie. Fuckin' pain in the ass. He was a good-looking cat so we'd have a good time at my discotheque—a lot of the fay chicks would go for his revolutionary bullshit, and if that was the program I'd come on with "Right on" and "Off the pig" good as Reggie. Shit, any way I get that pussy is all right with me. But then the dude started to lay heavy on me, like *caerme pesao.*

Reggie come on with, "You and my brother Earl are two of a kind—social parasites with no awareness of the revolutionary changes taking place around you. The Third World is on the march and you guys are going around hustling your own people. You and Earl are obsolete—there will be no hustlers in the new world. If you don't join the ranks of the oppressed then you'll be put up against the wall with the rest of them. You have no education, but that's no longer an excuse."

Always throwing that education shit in my face. "You're full of shit, Reggie. O-pressed, my ass, you been sucking Earl's titty all your life. He's the one that put you through school. Had you driving cars since you sixteen, dressed you sharp as a pimp, took care of business. Now you puttin' him down. I know what's got your head bad—I ain't so stupid, I know about Fanon and the Battle of Algiers and all that shit; I got the word from a brother in the Joint. You gonna kick over the man by shooting a few cops in the head? You crazy, that's what—they gonna bury you so fuckin' quick and nobody gonna even know you was a hero. What the fuck you care about the o-pressed? Take care of business; look out for number one—one way or the other there'll always be hustlers."

Earl, Earl, shoulda told you about your crazy brother, but I kept my mouth shut like usual and carried this cross around. One night, me and Reggie closed up my joint and then went over to this after-hours joint downtown Manhattan. Nearly all greaseballs that night. I was stoned, otherwise I'd never have gone there with this fuckin' Reggie. We was sitting at a table when we get a round of drinks from a table with around eight wise-guys. Valerio Mitri—a made-guy, underboss to Rocco's uncle, Dominick Cocozza—and company. Reggie says real loud, "We don't want no fucking drinks, take them back." Before I could say anything, Val Mitri came over. "I know you don't know me but I know your brother Earl."

"I'm getting sick and tired of hearing about my brother Earl—as far as I'm concerned he's a fuckin' Uncle Tom."

Val looked at me. I was stoned, what could I say, I smiled. This Reggie motherfucker is going to get me killed. Val went back and sat down at his table. Right away the joint is cleared out—my head was fogged—but I knew I had to do something. I stumbled over to Val's table. "Val, the kid don't mean no harm, he's high." Val's main gorilla, Buck, said, "We ain't mad, Carlito, these things happen." He stuck his hand out. Like a chump, I put my hand out. I was in a vise, couldn't move. Another gorilla grabbed me around the neck; I couldn't budge. But behind me I could hear feet like thrashing on the floor and I heard Reggie in a croak—"Carlito, Carlito"—I screamed, "Val, Val Mitri—Earl Bassey was breaking bread with Cocozza a few days ago—you know how much Rocco thinks of Earl—you know you have to kill me too—what are you going to say at the sitdown—that you killed his brother because he refused a drink? Think, Val, you ain't crazy, think!"

I got to him. He said, "*Basta.*" I heard puking; I knew it was Reggie. Jesus, his tongue must be strung out like a necktie.

"Get the shine out of here, Carlito—Buck ain't put hands on him yet." Buck. Buccia was a psycho, killed people with his bare hands, bit off noses; he weighed three hundred pounds but could jump over a bar like a fuckin' Doberman. I'd seen him in the east Harlem days. I was sobering up fast. "Val, you're doing the right thing, I'll get him out." Reggie was out—he had puke all over him. I dragged and carried him down the stairs. When I got him to the street, he come to, and what does he say? "Get your fucking hands off me, I can walk."

"You do just that, Reggie, take a fuckin' walk; you and me is parting ways."

He took off. I stood by the doorway of the joint trying to clear my head in the night air. Val came down with his crew. All of a sudden, Reggie came tearing around the corner in his car; he braked in front of the joint and started yelling, "Fuck all you guinea motherfuckers and fuck you, too, Carlito, you spic cock-sucker." Then he was gone.

I couldn't talk. Val said, "You see, Carlito, we give him a break, now we got trouble, on account of you sticking up for him. You see, you see!"

Yeah, I saw all right.

I didn't see Earl for a while after that. I didn't want to hassle with him over Reggie, I didn't want to tell him that Reggie had a watcha-call-it, complex, about him. I had Reggie figured—Earl is a man, a boss, uptown or downtown, where Reggie is a shitass and he knows it. Reggie don't want to be Earl's bro, he wants to be a big shot—dig me standing on my own two feet. Yeah, but you got athlete's feet, bro. He's going to do somethin' crazy, then jump into his grave—but let's not be in the hole with him, Earl, when he pulls the zipper up over hisself.

Earl called me. We met at Frank's Restaurant on 125th Street. He looked great, we rapped about old times. Then he told me, "Rocco gave me the word what Reggie did downtown—I know you went all the way for him, Carlito, even though he don't deserve it."

"He's your brother, Earl."

"I sent him back home, him and his two punks. He can't cut it—the slot is too big for him, he gags on it. The power is too much for him—I knew it in front but like he's my bro and I was hoping. Now I got to worry about these niggers robbing me when I ain't around."

"Reggie would have robbed you, Earl."

"I know that. I figure Lloyd is the man to run my thing. What do you think?"

"That's the man. Good business mind and bad on the street. But he's a gentleman moving around people; I dug him—he got style—good spender—rap with anybody—that's your man."

"What about you, Carlito?"

"Me? Shit, you crazy, Earl. I can't deal with them digits every day—bad numbers, runners robbing you, all that bookkeeping every day—I'd go crazy. Nah, that ain't my stick."

"Well, how about fronting for me? Lloyd can do the figures."

"That time is long gone, Earl. I'd have to kill me a spook every day. Look around you right here, some brother'll be bad-eyeing me. No good, you and me come up at a different time—these guys today don't want to hear that shit. I don't blame them. But Lloyd got to know that I'm with him a hundred percent; when they come to lean on him—and you know they got to try—he won't have to look around; I'll be there."

"I know that, Chas, I also know you boys'll be making your twice-yearly soon. Hip up, turkey, Uncle Sam wants you, and you gonna train in Atlanta, say twenty years."

"How you sound, colored boy?"

"I ain't jiving, Carlito, the handwriting's on the toilet wall. They ain't gonna let you out. Are you blind? These dudes is putting people on the moon; do you think they can't put the junk boys out of business? Where is your mental?"

"You know me, Earl; clean, baby, clean."

"You always was a crazy Po'Rican—I'm splitting for good soon, you know where to reach me in Saint Croix. If you ever need a job reference or somethin' that's where I'm at. Now get out my face."

And Earl was gone—and with a bundle. Was it possible for a hustler to make it and not pay his dues? I mean I heard about dudes running big joints like hotels and class restaurants in Miami and Vegas who made their bread racketeering but I never knew one close up. But here was Earl scuffling alongside me for twenty years— did time, been stabbed, been shot—come through all that and come out the other side with big bucks and retire clean. Unreal. Maybe that's the ticket for me too? Who you jiving? Shit, can't even be out of New York two weeks I go crazy. Some people get down on somethin' they want to go to the mountains or the woods—not me. I jump in my short—up the highway to 96th Street, then I cut through Harlem—junkies, whores, noise, fightin', garbage, fire escapes—that's me, that's reality. That's how I charge up again—clear my head, dig myself.

You ain't going nowhere, Carlito. You got people depending on you to live, people looking up to you, and like when you walk into a joint—no noise, cool, but everybody knows you're there. Carlito, *un bravo*. Right now, that's all there is. I don't understand living in the future—like Earl, doing this to get ready for that—who knows what's waiting on the corner? Could be an elephant gonna step on your back or a bullet up yo' ass. Stay loose, Carlito.

I don't put nothing in writing and the phone company has put more people in jail than cops, so I figured I'd heard the last of Earl. Lloyd Simpkins was a serious cat, I knew he could keep the thing together for Earl. Then Rocco sent for me. We met at a joint near La Guardia. First he gimme the good news—told me to get ready, that some big shipment was coming in and Vinnie would be around to see me. Then he gimme the bad news. "Something very bad is happening, Carlito. Someone put the snatch on Petey Amadeo's kid, Paul. They had him for two days. The old man put up a hundred thousand to get him back."

"What?"

"That's not the half of it. They were spades. Amadeo is a bug by nature but now he's going around biting himself—he brought in some old Sicilian who is supposed to keep a guy alive on a meat hook for days. And he sent for Nacho Reyes to come up from Miami. He doesn't want anyone to know. He wants to grab everybody at the same time."

"He's got a line on the guys, Rocco?"

"Yeah, the way I hear it—and I'm not supposed to know anything about this—but you're involved and I don't want you or Earl hurt—"

"What the hell you talking about?"

"Mr. A figures like this: his kid was snatched in front of his house; he'd just moved in—the only people that knew this were the people at my kid's christening. Now who was there? All wops except two spades and you— so he had Reggie checked out and Reggie fits right in with his two boys from Philly, Alfonso Lee and a guy called Shad."

"Well, that's his three right there."

"You don't know his mind, Charles. He figures Earl masterminded the whole scheme and since you're his boy, you're in on it too, and if you're not, then you go anyway so you won't get mad about Earl being taken out."

"Jesus Christ!"

"He's going to sweep all the pieces off the board."

"Hold the fuckin' phone! Rocco, what are we gonna do?"

"This Reggie and his two punks have to be buried— then we have a roundtable on you and Earl."

"Your uncle can do it, Rocco?"

"My uncle can do it, Carlito. The question is will he let us off the hook? Besides, my uncle is a very sick man."

"Us, Rocco?"

"Yeah, I'm in the jackpot too. Amadeo hates my guts—for many reasons. I've come up with a ready-made hook in my uncle. I've tried to use some finesse and my brains. I've tried to open up for the new groups, the Latins and the Blacks. Amadeo can't see this, he's a terrorist— with him it's kill and kill again. His solution to everything is a hit. So this beef now about his kid being snatched, when all are dead and buried he's going to blame the whole mess on me—I'm the one who opened up to the spics and niggers, I'm the one who is breaking with tradition—I'll be hit."

"That motherfucker! Let's whack him out first, Rocco—he bleeds! Then we check out."

"Use your head, Carlito; for once think with your head instead of your balls. Where would I go, where would I hide, some banana republic? I'll ride it out right here, and if not, so be it."

"Yeah, guess you're right, Rocco. Only the Cubans can run away—one place is as good as another to them. But if a P.R. jumps bail in Brooklyn, he runs away to the Bronx, and if a wop is deported he goes crazy. There's nothin' shakin' outside the U.S.A. You right."

"This is the way we'll deal: you will get to Nacho and his crew right away; you will con him that you got a good line on Reggie and that you're expecting word any minute—that will keep him off your back awhile. After Reggie is iced, Nacho will double back for you, but you'll be ready. By that time, my uncle can step in."

AND THAT'S THE WAY WE DEALT THE HAND. I COLLECTED all of my boys, including some who was like retired. Got all the hardware together and called for a meet with Nacho. He showed up in Harlem with two carloads of crazy Cubans (most of them dead now). They had pistols, sawed-off shotguns, and even hand grenades. All veterans from the Cuban shoot-outs, these kids didn't give a shit about nothin'. But my boys was all bad gangbusters too. There was no cause to rumble; I wanted to show Nacho I was talking from muscle, then I'd jive him Cuban-style. *"Mi hermano, mi par'na Nacho.* We must work together. We are after the three *niches* too. I know you're ready to do up Harlem and Bedford-Stuy to find them, but that ain't into nothin'. You can blow up all the black after-hours joints and you ain't gonna find them—you don't know what Reggie looks like, your *pistoleros* don't even speak English. *Ten calma,* Nacho, I'm expecting word any day now—I spread big bucks around with the *chibas,* then we grab all three. *Como te cae,* eh—you get first crack since you're the *echao pa'lante."* He dug it.

Then I got to Lloyd. "What the fuck I care if Reggie ripped off a couple of wops, Carlito? Ain't no skin off my ass."

"I'm gonna tell you one time, Lloyd, and you will believe me. The wops say me and Earl put Reggie up to the snatch. You're gonna say Earl ain't here. But when Earl hears they're gonna kill his brother he's gonna be here, and it's gonna be a bad motherfucker—won't be no tendin' to business. You and your boys gonna have to be in a war, and when the dust settles maybe Earl won't want to leave again and you got to get out that chair you're so comfortable in—and over who? Reggie? I know you'd piss on his grave in a minute, Lloyd. You gonna bleed over that motherfucker Reggie? You better give him up, Lloyd, he is a dead-ass, don't let's get weighed down with him. And what about me, Lloyd?

When they come for me you know I got to tell them where Earl is; they got a guy put you on a meat hook for days—you think they ain't gonna go down there and get Earl? There's only one way, Lloyd, and that's me coming up with Reggie in front: that'll show 'em that me and Earl was clean, that Reggie is an outlaw. You can find Reggie, Lloyd, you the only one can do this thing."

"What is Earl gonna say when he finds out I gave up his brother?"

"He's not gonna find out, Lloyd, no way—Nacho's got the contract. Since when you dealin' with the Cubans? You think I want Earl to know I put Reggie in the soup?"

"You comin' on too strong, Carlito, I need time to think."

"I'm thinking maybe you see both Reggie and Earl getting washed behind this thing and you walk away with all the fig newtons. If that's what you're thinking, Lloyd, I'll blow your motherfuckin' head off right here. Don't fuck with me, Lloyd; my balls is in the wringer and you turning the handle."

"I'll see what I can do."

"Do it, brother."

Alfonso and Shad were grabbed in Newark. Nacho and his boys delivered them to Amadeo on Long Island. Nacho told me this old Italian guy hung them on meat hooks in a walk-in freezer. Nacho said it was the worst scene he'd ever. From Nacho I believe it. Lloyd found out where these were for me and I gave them to Nacho, but Lee and Shad didn't know where Reggie was. Lloyd couldn't come up with Reggie and Reggie had the money—all of it. A week went by, no Reggie. The Cubans were running round the clock.

That Saturday morning I was closing up my disco joint when in walked Nacho and two of his goons, Camaguey and Paniagua. I was bullshitting Nacho about how I was expecting word on Reggie any day now when in came a kid ran errands for me, Squeaky. "Carlito, I just left the Village Gate with my girl—I saw him walking down to Houston Street, going in a building near the corner with some blonde chick."

"Why didn't you stay there and call up?"

"You always say never to talk on the phone, Carlito."

Nacho, who ain't supposed to understand English, said, *"El negro, eh? Vamos!"* I didn't go for moving with these three *Cubiches* alone but I had no choice. We barrel-assed down to that corner, parked, and waited. Everybody was packing—Nacho even had a silencer on his piece. We stood until daybreak, then this blonde came out the corner building. I jumped out of the car, waving my wallet like I had a shield—"Young lady, I'm Detective Velez from the safe-and-loft squad. We have that second floor under surveillance; were you stopped by my uniform man?"

"No sir, I came down from the third floor. I didn't see anyone."

"Okay, miss, sorry. You better hurry along—this is not a very nice neighborhood."

I got back in the car. "He's on the third floor—I'm sure that broad was with him." We waited until she was out of sight, then we piled out. In the hallway, Nacho started giving orders—"Camaguey, you cover the entrance to the building—Paniagua, you keep going up to the roof—Carlito and I will hit the apartments." Me and Nacho got to the third floor which was the top floor, the front pad was quiet so we eased to the back apartment—voices. I put my head down on the floor by the door—Reggie. The door was an old plank with a snap lock—I knew the kind from my B-and-E days, we hit the door together—wham! She come right off the hinges.

Reggie and Earl. They was sitting on a couch, one bulb overhead—a real skanky crash pad. "Freeze, mother-fuckers." Me and Nacho was both crouched like shoot-ers no sooner we hit that door. "Carlito, don't let him kill us," Earl yelled, his eyes on Nacho. *"Aguarda,* Nacho," I cooled Nacho. "You're supposed to deliver him alive." Earl said, "Let me explain—" " Too late, Earl, lights out. You cooked up this snatch—and of all people, Amadeo's kid—knowing that you was leaving me and Rocco hold-ing the bag—you knew these wops would cut us into little pieces. Reggie's a crazy nigger but you was always my man—how could you jap us like this, Earl?"

"You done fucked with m'dignity now, so kill me right here or hear me out."

"Cop your plea, Earl—*aguarda,* Nacho."

"I ain't copping no plea, motherfucker—I'm gonna tell you where it's at. The kid did it by himself with his two punks. I knew nothin' from nothin'—you gonna put me in a class with these crazy kids? Think, Carlito, is that me, is that my style? You think I'm out of my fuckin' mind? I been in Saint Croix. Reginald finally got to me yesterday, I flew in last night—look at the flight ticket in my pocket."

"*Qué pasa,* Carlito, *qué pasa?*" Nacho was getting annoyed. "*Espera,* Nacho. Earl, you my brother, the only one I ever had. I want to believe you—but Reggie got to go."

"Earl, they gonna put me on a meat hook"—Reggie was sweating bullets.

"You a fuck-up, but you my kid brother—you know you got to take me too, Carlito. Make your move, I'll understand."

"Earl, tell me what to do—you always tell me what I gotta do!" I was uptight.

"You got to off this dude alongside you and then we all split to the islands."

"No good, Earl, they're outside too—"

Then Reggie rolled the dice. He jumped and grabbed under a pillow of the couch—he got to pull the piece out—phft, phft—he took two in the back of the head splashing red right up in the air. Earl came straight for Nacho like a crazy man, screaming, "My brother, my brother!" Nacho smoked again—Earl stumbled in his tracks, then went down on his face right at our feet. Nacho pointed his piece at Earl's head—then, without even knowing why, I put my pistol to Nacho's temple.

"You know I will blow the top of your brains out, Nacho."

"*Es un moyete.*"

"*Es mi hermano,* Nacho—I owe him too much."

"*Estás loco,* Carlito."

"I'll take my chances—you leave now, there's been noise here; take the car and beat it before the bulls get here. Take Paniagua and Camaguey."

"*Los Italianos*—"

"You contracted for three, you delivered three—case closed. If they find out about Earl being here today, that's my worry, they all look alike to you. Why should you and I kill each other over these fuckin' Italianos? Let me do it my way."

Paniagua and Camaguey appeared at the door. They said, "Nacho, people opening doors, the *camarónes* will be here any minute. *Vamos a echar un pie.*"

Nacho picked up his shells from the floor.

"*Vamos andando,*" he said; as be got to the door he turned smiling at me. "I could kill you now but I do not choose to—your loyalty to your friend is a rare thing in this business. I am impressed—but it will get you killed. At your funeral I will say, he was a loyal friend, crazy, but loyal. *Adiós,* Carlito."

"*Adiós,* Nacho."

And they split. I got Earl to Beekman Hospital in a taxi. He was hit in the stomach and in bad pain but he could hear me. "Give me your wallet, Earl, don't have no identification on you—tell them your name is Johnson, Earl Johnson. I'll keep tabs on you that way while you're in the hospital—nobody will know you were in New York—then you can hop a plane home."

"My brother, Carlito—"

"Forget about him, Earl, he's gone. He was bad news from the get go—everybody told you—and he had a bad attitude for you; he was gritty but he was greedy and he'd of got us all killed. You did more than enough for him, mark it paid—you got your family to think about."

I carried him to the door of the emergency entrance. "This far as I go, Earl. There may be cops in there. I don't want no static now—you was drinking, you ended up in the Village, you was mugged, had your wallet taken, you put up a fight and got shot, got it?"

"Thanks, ol' buddy."

"I'll have a broad down here to visit you, whatever you need. Catch you later."

Never seen either of them cats again. Earl made it back to Saint Croix and got out of all the shit. You entitled, Earl. Nacho finally ran out of luck. He got whacked out in Miami. Nacho was in a joint, coked to the gills—this young kid who Nacho hardly knew came in complaining to Nacho that his girl had been abused. Nacho went out to the parking lot and these thugs shot him in the head. Didn't even know who he was and didn't care. Jesus, Nacho Reyes—unbelievable.

8

I TOOK A PLANE TO PUERTO RICO. JUST TO GET AWAY FROM all the hassle and shooting going on in New York. I heard Prohibition was a bitch, but the dope rumbles sure has buried a lot of people in my time. I got a small room in a guest house in Isla Verde, stayed out of the fancy hotels and late-night joints. I wanted to rest up and I wasn't carrying no piece and didn't want to run into no half-bad-ass looking for a rep. So I just lay around the beaches—no shave, just a pair of shorts—my head got together. Then I teamed up with this fox from Ohio. She was a schoolteacher and into the hippie scene but she was a knocked-out-looking broad—blonde hair, green eyes. Here was me, with no diamond pinkie ring and walkin' around in my drawers and sneakers, making time with this doll. This new scene was really somethin'. I guess I was born too early—all this protest shit can't be all bad if it's made all these freaky heads available.

Her name was Gail or Gale. She was a real American type—anglowasp bit—but she was all shook up about

Vietnam and the poor and worried about the lettuce and the grapes in California and all that bullshit—unbeliev-able—but looking as good as she was I went right along. I told her I was with the poverty program in New York and doing a lot of work on my own time with the Lords and with spade gangs, and I'd rap about commitment and orientation like a welfare dude. We flew to Saint Thomas, then we chartered a boat and just bummed around. Beef, Trunk, Drake's Anchorage, Virgin Gorda—all the islands for a couple of weeks. A Hollywood scene starring me and Gail. She smoked grass and I'd smoke a joint with her, but I told her I was against all drugs and that she should put that scene behind her on account of dope was a drag on the revolution. Lordy.

I was in love—again. She was into music. I got her some of the Sinatra ballad albums and we'd get high and goof behind them—she was young but Frank can talk to anybody. "My Way" is Paul Anka's song for Sinatra; on a night when we was real cozy anchored off Saint John's we got to rapping about favorite songs and I told Gail this song has a special message for me and if she could dig the song, she could dig me—the moon was out and we went into a great clinch. *Qué* party!

I put in a call to New York and got the word that every-thing was okay by Rocco, come home right away. Me and Gail flew back to San Juan—I bought her an outfit all in white—she had a heavy tan. When she got all dolled up to go out that night she looked like a movie star. Like to fall out when I saw her. I ain't a profane cat, but I had to say, "Thank you God, for them fine chibs." Of course,

I was clean m'self. You must be doing somethin' right, Carlito, here you are pushing your forties, nearly everybody is in jail or been wasted, and here is you still out there with a young thing on your arm. You devil! It was our last night. We caught the show at the Tropicoro. Damn if it wasn't Paul Anka hisself. We had to be at ringside although it cost me a yard. He sang our song, we drank champagne, held hands—shit, ain't no more after this. Like Gail would say, groovy.

After the show, we wandered into the casino; gambling is not my bag but Gail wanted to shoot a hand. Bad news. No sooner I walked into the casino Cesar come over to us. Cesar was an old Harlem boy—he'd been a knockaround guy as a kid but he'd been straight for years, been working as a croupier in P.R. and now was an assistant manager in the casino. He'd made it the hard way and I gave him a lot of credit.

"Carlito, I'm in trouble. I need your help. Walberto and Monchin—you know them, from the 103rd Street crowd—been running a murder game on me. I won't okay their credit—they are beaters—so last night they got real heavy on me, tried to gorilla me with a piece. I can't deal with these motherfuckers, Carlito—you know my job here. Can you straighten them out for me? I hate to bother you but I got a family now."

He's worried about his family—who's worried about me? Jesus! What am I, the fuckin' Red Cross?

"Okay, Cesar, I'll hang around awhile; maybe I can talk some sense to these guys."

Gail had a funny look on her face. I guess she got the picture real quick-like—the money, the clothes on me now, the wise-guy talk.

I told her, "Wait in the lobby for me, Gail. If anything happens, you don't know me—don't get involved. Otherwise, I'll be with you in a little while." She split and I hung around the crap table.

In walked Walberto and Monchin. Walberto was white and Monchin was black, so people would laugh when they said they was brothers, but they was really cousins. They were all duded up in tuxedos and patent leather so they must have made a score in New York. Never seen one without the other—two lightweights, but Monchin was sneaky fast and would hurt you. Walberto was the slicker of the two but he was jive. If you got to him Monchin would go along.

"*Ola*, Carlito—wha's happening, my man! Monchin, dig who's here—Carlito."

"I got a beef with you, Walberto, let's go to the back of the room."

The three of us went to a back corner of the casino—place was crowded but nobody was paying us any mind.

"*Qué pasa, mi hermano?* Monchin and me always been tight with you, Carlito, why you sounding us?"

I was rapping to Walberto but I had my eye on Monchin, who probably had the piece.

"Cesar is my man in P.R.—now you gonna come here from out of town to gorilla my man here. You crazy? Don't you know there are heavy people into this casino—

and you gonna come in here with a rice-and-beans shake-down? Back off, motherfucker, and tell your brother not to be bad-eyeing me, because if he makes a move you gonna get the first shot in the face and my people here will take care of the rest—okay?"

"*Coño,* Carlito, I'm surprised that you should say that about us—me and Monchin always look out for Cesar—he's one of the boys. I'm surprised—right, Monchin?"

"Yeah, Berto, Cesar's our boy."

"Then it must be a misunderstanding. Come here, Cesar. Cesar, the boys say it is a misunderstanding, a breakdown in the communication; they didn't mean no harm, they ain't gonna bother you. However, Cesar, if you see the boys around town in any joint you send them a bottle right away—do the right thing, okay?"

I shoulda been a diplomat. That's me, always trying to straighten things out without nobody getting hurt and everybody making a dollar. But what do I get, a bum rep as a troublemaker, that's what they say about me. Fuck 'em.

My girl was waiting in the lobby.

"I left, Charley, but I came back."

"Why?"

"Charley, you've been playing a part for me and it wasn't necessary. I don't like to be made a fool of."

"Listen, Gail, what am I supposed to tell you, that I'm a hoodlum? What's the point? I didn't ask you where you came from or where you're going. I'm only interested in the Gail standing in front of me; I couldn't care less what you did in Lawrence, Ohio."

"Lorain, Charley—Lorain, Ohio."

"That's what I said, Lorain, Ohio. Yeah, I consorted with known criminals—uh—bad guys—when I was a kid, but that's in the past—in the new world that don't mean nothin'. As far as me being in the socio bag, Gail, I ain't jiving you, I been helping people in the ghetto— why, just the other day, this cat got stabbed on 111th Street, I took him to the hospital even though the seats in my Lincoln got full of blood—that's typical of me. Like a goodwill ambassador—here tonight a working man was being abused by these two thugs, I intervened and prevented a problem. People don't give you credit for things like that. I can't believe that you'd walk out on me without giving me a chance to explain what it's like to come up in a jungle."

These socio broads always go heavy for that shit about the jungle. I had to pull out all the stoppers—I wasn't gonna forfeit my last piece on my last night, looking good as she was. Gawd, she was a doll.

"Charley, we have Puerto Ricans in Lorain; I know what your people have to go through. Look, let's forget it—let's just have some fun."

Well all right. And fun we had. She had me dancing to rock music at the Hunca Munca, then we danced at the El Chico, then we hit Annando's, Danny's, the Wine Cellar, drunk on one another—gonna play the string out. Don't know if it was the booze or what but Gail was getting misty-eyed and wouldn't let go of me.

"Charley, what about us? Is there any chance something can come of us? I don't know whether it's the beauty of these islands or what, but I've never felt this way before. Will I ever see you again?"

You know I was stoned because I got noble and didn't put down no spiel—I leveled with her, guess I had a feeling for her I didn't realize.

"I don't know, Gail. I'm into some bad scenes. My life ain't tropical beaches and sunny skies—in the city it's different, it's asphalt and gray and busted windows—I'm different. I move around a lot, get into hassles. You ain't ready for that, and because I go for you, I'm telling you in front. Believe me, if I had anything to offer you, I'd never let you go. But I know myself—I get restless, I'd hurt you. I'm poison, Gail—don't get mixed up with me."

We was both cryin' in our champagne. It was great. Then we went to her hotel room and had each other for breakfast, lunch, and dinner. *Qué jéva!*

That evening she went with me to the airport. I didn't want her to, she insisted. I told her to stay in the cab and go back to the hotel, but she got out. I got a flight on standby. We had a few minutes just holding hands in the middle of the terminal, not saying anything. Then I could see the tears.

"Let go, Gail. It's for the best."

Those pretty green eyes were flooding now. I was wishing I could say something to her, for her. Like my life is a garbage can, I'm a street fighter, a dope pusher, even been a pimp—get away, girl, don't get into my mess, I ain't gonna be around long. But I said, "Tell you what, baby, write down your home address and telephone, I'll get in touch with you next week after I've taken care of some business. Then I'll fly out to see you or I'll have you fly into New York and you can stay with me—we'll give it a try, how's that?"

"You mean it, Charley?"

"Have I ever lied to you?" I lied.

She wrote her address down on a piece of paper and pressed it into my hand—all this fuss over a mug like me. Unbelievable.

My plane was leaving. "Okay, Gail, no more tears, you're gonna have me crying—now you turn around and start walking, you got a great wiggle. That's the first thing I dug about you—c'mon, lemme see you wiggle away."

I watched her all the way to the end of the terminal until she was gone. Then I let the paper out of my hand onto the ground.

Adiós, rubia. I got on the plane dragging my ass low. I didn't know why but that night my way didn't seem so hot. Like I was unsure of myself, my way of life—bad vibes, man, bad vibes. I shoulda listened. And like always when things is so bad they can't get worse—wha' happen? They get worse.

9

So THEY HAD THEIR SITDOWN OVER THE REGGIE AFFAIR.
Rocco was my mouthpiece. The joint was Messina's
Restaurant in guinea Brooklyn around Bath Beach,
Gravesend Bay. The jukebox was playing "Mala Femina"
so right away I knew I was in trouble. Me and Rocco sat
at the bar.

"Don't be nervous, Carlito, they're not going to shoot
anyone at a roundtable—this is neutral ground, like a
court-martial in the army."

"I ain't in the army, Rocco."

"Neither am I, and that's part of our trouble."

"Wadda you mean, Rock?"

"I mean I've not been made. I never went for this pro-
tocol shit. My only interest was making money; I don't
want to be a tough guy talking about this hit and that hit.
And I've made more money for the outfit than all of them
put together, so I've been independent and walked away
from this made-guy business—and now I'm in trouble."

"Wadda you mean, Rock?" Jesus Christ!

"I mean Uncle Dom is dying, cancer. Amadeo is acting boss—this guy Mario Battaglia is like an underboss; my rabbi is fading, Charles, and for the first time I need rank—everybody is getting promoted except me."

"Wadda you give a shit about this captain-and-general shit, Rocco? Make the money."

"They'll whack me out, Carlito. Mr. A cannot stand my guts; he knows I've been going around him to Uncle Dom for years. When my uncle goes, I'm in trouble."

"These people got to be crazy, with the money you've made for them!"

"That's the only thing I got going for me."

"Well, you got me and my guns going for you."

"I know that, Carlito, but it's not that simple."

I'd never seen Rocco so down. Then that fucking "Mala Femina" playing—that's got to be the background music on all the F.B.I. tapes. I was shook up. Then to improve things around this time in stashes Mr. Petcy A and his traveling kangaroo court of the ugliest spitters I ever did see. Two gorillas in front, two flanking Amadeo, and two bringing up the rear. They marched straight through the bar into a back room. Everybody in the joint was examining their glass all of a sudden like a freeze—the little wop scared the shit out of everybody, including me. *Madonna!*

Then Cocozza came in with Valerio Mitri, Buccia, and this guy Battaglia. Yea, team!—'til I got a look at Uncle Dom—a dead man—his skull was coming out through his skin, he couldn't have weighed a hundred pounds. His voice was a croak, "Hello, Rocco—I see you got your Spanish friend here. *Como está,* Carlo?"

"Okay, Mr. Cocozza, okay—glad to see you."

The back room had a long table with a short table crossing it at the end like a *T*. There were three chairs at the short table; they were empty when we came into the room, everybody was sitting at the long table. I said, "What about bugs, Rocco?"

"Don't worry, we got a guy checked it out this afternoon."

"If I had m'druthers, we'd be out in the bay talking underwater—these guys look like conspiracies all by themselves. Jeez!"

Then these three old guys walked in. Everybody got up—me too. What is this jive? The pope, the three kings—what am I doing here? Dom Cocozza and Amadeo was kissing and embracing with the King Cole trio; they were rapping in Sicilian—"*Pietro,*" "*Domenico,*" "*Don Cesare.*" *Don Fangula,* sez me. The three wise men sat down at the small table facing us. Reminded me of my first bust down in the old special sessions. The guy in the middle was an active boss—old, gray on top, but dap in the dark suit with a shoulder fit that had to go for three yard. It took him five minutes to take off his hat, gloves, and topcoat—with everybody standing up. Everything he had on seemed cut from the same material. This guy had to be a general, for low.

Cesare Mazzone, also known as Chick Mason. All these Italians was Irish prizefighters in the thirties. The two old guys flanking Mazzone—Mustache Petes—had the shirt buttoned to the top but no tie—rumpled black suits and puffing on guinea stinkers. They was old dons, but their faces said Don't fuck with me.

I ain't ever felt good inside a courtroom. Mazzone opened up sounding like Wallace Beery with a sore throat.

"Awright, wad is the beef here, wad's the problem here? Lemme hear from Pete first."

Pete Amadeo. Short, squat, dark with like nappy hair. Maybe some club members swam across from Africa to Sicily way back when. He had a bad-news face, the kind you ain't gonna stop and ask Where's the Woolworth Building? Stays mad. Maybe he's right—he stayed alive through a whole lot of wars.

"The beef is that I'm out one hundred large. Three niggers put the snatch on my boy Paulie, and I had to buy him back. One of them was Earl Bassey's brother, Reggie, and he got the line on Paulie from the time he came to Rocco's house with Earl and with this mutt Carlito, here."

Rocco grabbed my arm—steam was coming out my ears.

Cocozza stepped up. You could hardly hear him but everybody listened. Ol' Dom was very respected. He made his bones in Sicily as a kid—when he came here in the twenties he was already a man of respect. He'd whacked out his share but he was known to have a cool head and a good rap. Dom said,

"Good evening, Don Cesare, Don Peppino, Don Nicola. Before we get into what happened with the money, I think I ought to say that this kid Carlito is here on his own hook—nobody brought him here. He came because Rocco asked him to, because he's doing the right thing. I admit he's a Spanish kid, but he can't help that— he's trying to do the right thing. I don't think we should kick off this meet by insulting him, Pete."

Pete said, "Everybody knows I got all the respect in the world for you, Dom, but you got the wrong slant on this thing; your nephew Rocco has sold you on the niggers and the spics and that's crazy. This thing of ours been doing okay without these people. Why do we have to do business with them? Why do we have to open up for them? You give them a break—what happens? They put the snatch on you. I say freeze them out—anybody gets out of line, whack him out right on his front stoop. And you listen to Rocco, Dom, and yet twice he's been asked in and twice he's walked away—is that the right thing? I mean, am I right or wrong?"

I could see Cocozza got hot—his face got white, his eyes got small—but his voice come up strong; you could see old Dom was a man of *cojones* in his day.

"Pietro Amadeo, when you talk about my kid nephew you talk about me. If a man ain't ready to be made, he ain't ready—that don't mean he can't do a good job. You know Rocco is the best man in your whole fucking crew—maybe he ain't out there waving his pistol at waiters like some of the young punks you got right in this room—he's using his brain and making money, that's what he's doing. Half of these tough guys you give them a contract and they shit in their pants. I know what Rocco can do because I've sent him myself. And you, Pete, have you forgotten what I am to you that you don't give me respect? I'll go out in the fucking alley with you right now and we can kill each other."

Pete got shook up here.

"No, Dom, I didn't mean I got no respect—"

Chick butted in here.

"Take it easy, Dom, you know Pete says things, but he don't mean no harm."

But Dom was hot. Go get 'im!

"No, I've had it up to here with your bad mouth, Pete. I took you off a cattle boat with holes in your pants—I put you behind one of my trucks and bought you your first suit. You forgot that, huh, Pete? And the time of the Castellammarese you went with Joe the Boss. You bet on the wrong horse that time, right, Pete? Who got you out of town when Maranzano said you was to be hit? Who got the okay from Charley Lucky so you could come back? *Cretino*—you owe me your life—and I should live to hear you insult my family—you scumbag!"

I was scared shitless by now. These wops are crazy. What am I doing here?

I could see Pete was stunned. Everybody was very nervous by now. Even the two old dons had stopped sucking on their stogies.

Chick Mason said, "Take it easy, Dom, take it easy— we ain't gonna get nowhere talking about old beefs. What's the story about Pete's money, Dom? That's what we gotta straighten out."

"All right, Cesare, the story is, yeah, Reggie Bassey and two black punks snatched Paulie, but they was all hit right away, and the Spanish kid came up with them. Are we gonna blame Carlito and Earl Bassey for what three crazy punks did? You know how these kids are today, Cesare—you can't talk to them. Look at some of our kids—good Italian blood being lost right here in Brooklyn in crazy cowboy shit, and even stool pigeons. I mean these kids got no respect nohow.

"Now, we gonna blame Rocco too because he got friends with the Blacks and the Spanish? Cesare, we got to move with the times—the holy Church stays on top, right? Why the Church stay on top? Because the pope and the cardinals they see the handwriting on the wall. Times change, they change—make a cardinal here, one there. Move with the times. We gotta do the same. You do not fight history, you learn from it. We can live with these new groups—we can make money with them. These younger guys can't, but you and me, Cesare, we remember when we was the niggers here. I mean, am I right or wrong?"

Chick and the two dons went into a huddle. Then Chick said, "I wanna hear from this Spanish kid."

Oh shit. I almost said Yes, your honor.

"Right here, Mr. Mason," says me.

"Where's the money?"

"I don't know. The first two, Fonso and Shad, said Reggie had it all. Nacho and me had to waste Reggie quick—he went out on us before we could find out where the money was. It couldn't be helped, he was shooting at us like crazy."

"Where's Earl Bassey?"

"I don't know that either, Mr. Mason. Earl took off long before this happened. I think he was worried about the feds and he wanted to retire and get away from it all— you know, one of them numbers."

"Don't give me that nigger talk; you ain't no nigger— that's the trouble with you spics, you don't know what you are. Some of them even look like Chinese, so help me. Now you listen to me, Carlo—I don't believe a fuckin' thing you're sayin', but we're gonna let it slide because we can't prove different right now. But we'll check it out and if you come up wrong we'll stick your head in a bucket of acid, *capisce?*"

"I got you, Mr. Mason."

"Now tell me the truth, if you knew where Bassey was would you tell us?"

"No, I wouldn't."

"Well, at least you ain't no stool pigeon. Dom, here's how it's gonna be: Rocco stays in business but he owes Pete the money. Pete, you'll apologize to Dom for hurting his feelings. Dom, you'll go along with Pete—what the hell, you guys go back too far to fall out over a couple of shines. Rocco, you listen to Pete—don't go running to your Uncle Dom over every little shit. And you, you fuckin' Puerto Rican—you watch your ass, don't try to be a smart guy. Awright, enough of this bullshit. Bring me the cook over here, I wanna put in a special order of calamari for everybody."

They put on a feed that was out of sight. They may be crazy but they sure eat good. Then they started telling war stories about who had to shoot his brother, his mother—how the mob wasn't the same, the new kids were a bunch of faggots, like that. The party broke up late; me and Rocco were leaving together when over comes Mario Battaglia, big smile—"Rocco, I wuz wid you all the way—put it there, Carlito, I heard you was a stand-up guy and now I believe it."

Me and Rocco shook hands with Battaglia. He was a made-guy with a lot of balls—Pete liked him and he was moving up fast in the outfit. Then he said, "Listen, Rocco, I want in on that next order of yours coming in but you don't have to say nothin' to Pete about it." Me and Rocco were surprised but Rocco said, "Okay, Mario, you're in." Me, I didn't say nothin', I know I didn't say nothin'.

Rocco drove me to midtown where my car was. "Talk about a kangaroo court, Rocco—that's a hell of a legal system you guys got."

Rocco laughed—"You got a fair trial, didn't you?"

"Listen, Rocco, they didn't give me my rights and that fuckin' judge, Chick Mason, he'll shoot you first then find you guilty later. Unbelievable."

We drove awhile, then Rocco said, "The whole thing's falling apart, Carlito."

"Wadda you mean, Rock?"

"I mean the mob is falling apart. These guys like Chick, my uncle, they're dinosaurs. When they go, there won't be anyone to replace them."

"But there's always someone who'll take a shot, Rock."

"It's not the same; the new kids aren't as hungry, for obvious reasons—they're in school, they got jobs—a wise-guy is made on the streets catching hell. He can't learn his trade in suburbia. Then there's the government with the bugs. The electronics have knocked the jock off us. You can't talk anywhere, we're all paranoid—there's guys don't want to be bosses, imagine, for fear of the heat. Then the feds are on our ass twenty-four hours a day— they put a team on you, put you to bed, get up with you, follow you into the restaurants, the fights, the bars, checking your tabs, checking your kids in school. They got a bug into Sonny's house while they were laying the foundation, they got a bug into Patriarca's office. Then you got stool pigeons inside the mob—Vinnie Teresa in New England, Joe Cago right here in New York."

"How could that be, Rock?"

"A lot of reasons—some of the bosses have been too greedy, sitting on top of millions—meanwhile the soldiers are starving. New attitudes—every man for himself, no loyalty. This country will corrupt anything, even the mafia."

"Wadda you gonna do?"

"What am I going to do, Charles? What can I do? I've got both feet over the edge of the roof now, there's no turning back. I'm going straight down—maybe I'll grab a clothesline here and there but that won't hold me. Can't run, can't hide, so just keep going till I break my neck. Maybe you should have let those guys throw me off the roof on 107th Street."

"Your ass! If I know you, you probably would have landed on a pile of twenties and walked away with the bread."

Rocco snorting and getting high. I didn't like it but like fuck it. That's my main trouble. I don't worry enough. I always get the right vibes, the knot in the gut, the chill in the back of the neck, just like anybody else, but the trouble with me is I don't stop, I wanna come out the other side anyway. I see the stop sign and I wanna press on the pedal. Like when I was a kid I'd race a bike through the tunnel on Park Avenue against the light or I'd hang from the roof with one hand. And didn't need no audience. I been my own spectator like there was two of us—watcha gonna do next, Carlito? That kind of scene. But I ain't crazy and I ain't got no death wish. That kind of bullshit pisses me off. The shrinks always give you that, you wanna be punished, you wanna be caught—garbage. Who the hell wants to go to jail? You really gotta be crazy. They don't understand that the hustler's got confidence. That's the key, confidence. The hustler's got the confidence he can pull it off, he's coming out the other side okay. When he's up on a roof looking at apartments he's confident no cop is gonna put a bullet up his ass when he's on the fire escape. And he's confident no cop or the owner is gonna stop him when he's carrying a twenty-one-inch Motorola down the street in broad daylight. And he's confident he can walk through Kennedy Airport with a kilo strapped to his back.

Ain't nobody more surprised than a hustler when he's popped. Damn, what's going on here, how did this happen? The shrinks has been conned—been psyched by the clients. Ha, the dope pusher's got it all doped out. I am the master of this field too. Many is the time in the Joint that I have worked out a man's legal problem and then I have gotten to his skull and "That's where your head is at" and the dude has gotten shook up—"Damn, Carlito, how'd you do it? That's it, that's where my head is at." The public don't know it, but there's plenty heavy thinkers in the Joint and there ain't no better place for heavy rapping and thinking, except that most of them are only worried about their own writs and briefs. The government ought to start up a think tank in the Joint—I'll bet they come up strong. Yeah, a think-tank tank.

10

WELL, NOW WE'RE GETTING DOWN TO MY LAST CON-
spiracy. I was busy fixing up my discotheque, trying to
make it like a joint from the speakeasy days—Bonnie
and Clyde jazz. What with all the straights dressing up
like Al Capone, I figured this was the ticket. I got a lot
of ideas about things like that. Anyway, Rocco's man
Vinnie dropped by one night. In all the years I known
Vinnie, I never got his last name. The bulls never believe you, but in the life you can know a guy for twenty
years and never know his last name. And if he's a wop,
God forbid you should ask—automatically you're a
stoolie. Funny. Anyway, Vinnie walks in, points to the
john, and says, "Let's go for a blow." I got mad at this—
I did not allow no snorting in my joint. Fuckin' people
got no consideration for a man's living. "Vinnie, you
know I'm very strict about my rule, let's go round the
block." So we went for a walk around the block. Good
candy too. The sphinx speaks, "Get your money together, then double it—yeah, double it. It's already

left—should be here by Friday, Saturday—I'll be
around. Fifties and hundreds."

"Wait a minute, Vinnie. Double—that's long bread—
way out—I don't know if I can make it—"

"That's your lookout. You in or you out?"

"Okay, I'm in—I'll get it together."

"Saturday."

"You got it. That's good snort, Vin, you got some
more?"

"See ya."

Two hundred thou. That means the pot is two mill.
That means two hundred keys. Must be coming over in
a trailer truck. Good God almighty damn, biggest move
I ever heard of—you know I'm dealing myself in. The
government declares war, all the pushers run for their
holes—meanwhile the panic sets in, the price goes up,
up, up. Then the real hustlers grab hold and make the real
scores.

I'm scuffling around all week getting my money together. Friday, the *France* docked. Well all right. But
Saturday, no Vinnie; Sunday, no Vinnie. I knew we were
in trouble, I knew it in front, but I hung in anyway. That's
when the hustler pays his dues, when he don't know how
he's gonna get zapped—he knows the rug pulled out from
under but he don't know how or where or who. That is a
bitch, when you're waiting. You know the feds are out
there scheming, but you don't know who they got, or
what they got, or who's talking, or whether they been
staked out next door for a month. But you know yo' ass
is up for grabs. You know it, motherfucker.

I ain't left the house for two days. Monday night I can't
sit no more. I go to my discotheque—I was calling it
Bonnie 'n Clyde; it was really shaping up with live music
and everything. Around 3 A.M., the phone rang behind
the bar. "Carlito, for you." It was Rocco. "Close up and
wait for me." Click. Jesus Christ! Maybe the wops got
him and I'm gonna be hit. I chased everybody out the
joint. Then I ran down to the basement and got a sawed-
off shotgun and a Walther PPK automatic I had behind
a vent. I put the piece under the cash register and the
shotgun at the far end of the bar—the way I was going if
I had to make a fast exit. Better call uptown for some of
my people. Hold the phone—maybe the feds got Rocco
and they're coming for me, and me with all this hardware.
I must be out to lunch in my skull. I ran downstairs and
hid all the artillery again. By now I was in a cold sweat—
like I said, it's a bitch when you don't know what's coming off. But Rocco would never give me up—what
happened to Vinnie? All the lights were out; I sat behind
the bar and poured myself a stiff shot. Car lights outside,
then I heard Rocco—"Carlito, open up." So be it.

He was all fucked up. I never seen Rocco this way—
scuffed, no shave, all shook up. "Trouble, Carlito,
trouble."

"Jesus Christ, Rocco, what's up?"

"The shit is down in a station wagon under the highway—been there since Friday."

"So what happened?"

"This French kid, Marcel, drove it off the ship; Vinnie
got in with him—they got as far as Canal Street to go to

the tunnel. Then they bailed out. Vinnie got to a phone—he said where he left the car and that they'd been made by the feds. The two of them have disappeared, but there's no arrest."

"So what the fuck is going on, Rocco?"

"Battaglia got to me tonight. He says his two hundred large came from Amadeo and that I have to account for it plus the hundred from the Reggie mess. But that money is already gone with my own three hundred as front money. I put up five hundred thou!"

"But where's Vinnie—he's gotta account."

"Battaglia said don't worry about Vinnie, I'm responsible for Amadeo's money. My uncle is in a coma since last week—he's going out for sure, they know it. Can you believe this?"

"We're in trouble, we're in trouble."

"I'm ruined, Carlito. I have to account for their three hundred and I've blown my own three hundred. I'm dead, Carlito, I'm dead."

Rocco slumped on a stool. The joint was pitch-black but I could see he ain't slept for days. He was at the end of the line.

"What'll we do, Carlito, what'll we do?"

The brains have failed, now comes time for the balls!

"We gotta get that car."

"Are you crazy? The feds are waiting."

"Vinnie may have panicked, Rocco, and even if the feds made the car—if a good driver gets the jump on them he can get away. You remember that guy, Bobby Iggione?"

"Yeah, Bobby Higgins—they were waiting and he still got away—that was in the fifties."

"I'm down."

"You're crazy, Charles."

"You got a suggestion, Rocco?"

"I'm wasted."

"Okay. First, we'll take a dry run in my car, shoot past the station wagon, check out the scene—then we double back in your car. Wait a minute, Rocco, how am I going to get the car going? Got no time to be crossing wires."

"I got a duplicate set of the keys when the money went down."

"Well all reet! We'll come barrel-assing down, you brake, I'll roll out—you take off south, I'll cut east on Canal. I know the area like my hand. I'll run them sombitches into the ground—they won't catch me."

"But—"

"Ain't no butts here 'cept ours, what we is trying to save, Rock. If Amadeo says you gotta go, how far behind am I gonna be? I say roll the dice."

"You're on."

I felt better already. Waiting around is a drag, but once you make up your mind what's to be, it's easy. Action is where I'm at.

IT WAS AROUND 4 A.M., NO MOON—LIKE THE P.R.'S SAY, darker than a poor man's hopes. We drove both our cars to 23rd Street near the Hudson River. Then Rocco parked his car and got in with me. I drove south under the West Side Highway. We were moving downtown on West Street when on our left we passed the Federal House of Detention. Of all the buildings in the world to see tonight, we gotta see the fuckin' federal jailhouse. *"Madon,"* said Rocco. *"Bendito,"* said me. We were approaching Canal Street—I was clocking lights so the red light would catch us on Canal Street. We caught the light. There it was under the overpass, second car down, facing east. A Volkswagen bus. Four hundred pounds, eighty million fuckin' dollars in those side panels. The sweat was coming down my back into my ass.

Not a livin' ass in sight, stone quiet, nothing moved. That means there's forty agents around here. The light turned green—we went down to Chambers, made a left, went east a few blocks, then back up to 23rd Street where Rocco's car was.

Nobody on our tail. Ha. We got into Rocco's four-door Caddie. He was driving, I was in the back laying on the floor, facing the left door. Rocco said, "Bobby Higgins crashed into the cars, drove all over sidewalks—you ready for that, Carlito?" "No I'm down here on the floor knocking off a piece of tail. C'mon, Rocco!"

"You know what they told Bobby Higgins?"

"What?"

"The feds can only put you in jail, but you know what we're gonna do—that's what they told him."

"So he went, right?"

"Yeah, he had to, but you're not in the same jackpot, Carlito."

"The hell I ain't, Rocco! Amadeo's got a double-decker coffin ready for the two of us. Now listen, no sense trying to sneak up on them—you barrel-ass, hit your brake when my rear door is on a line with the driver's side of the bus—I'll dive into the street and roll right up to the door of the bus and jump in. Do me one thing, Rocco—jump out of your car for a second, stand up, then jump back in and drive like hell, make a lot of noise. They'll think you came for the junk, got cold feet, and took off. They'll come after you like gangbusters."

"Meanwhile, you'll tippy-toe out with the bus, right?"

"Sounds terrific, don't it, Rocco?"

"You're out of your mind."

We came back down on West Street. I had the door cracked.

Rocco said, "We're coming to Canal Street, I'm stepping on the gas—get ready!"

He slammed on the brakes—I dove out to the street with the keys in my hand. I heard Rocco yelling, then he took off. All hell broke loose, like the Fourth of July—lights, whistles, sirens, cars screeching and braking, gunfire. Don't ask me how, but I got into the bus and got it started. *La puta madre*—let's roll. I shot across West Street right into a garage on the corner of Canal. At least three cars came running out right at me. I cut left hard, bounced off a gas pump, then with my foot on the floorboard I cut east on Canal. The agents' cars were swarming all over me by the dozens—we was banging and crashing all over. They was hitting me from the back and the side like fuckin' kamikaze. But I still had the four wheels down on the ground, still running east on Canal; then I saw a helicopter coming at me when I was getting near the entrance to the Holland Tunnel. Blam! They blew my windows out—the bus jumped in the air, but I kept going. The chopper was bumping me with the pontoons trying to tip me over. *Madre puta!* Canal Street is wide open—I need a roof. On Varick Street I made a hard right, jumped a sidewalk, and went through a space in the wall of the exit ramp of the Holland Tunnel. Wrong way—fuck it! I was out of my skull—I barreled into the tunnel with the cars coming out. Move over, I'm coming on. I was bouncing off the walls of the tunnel, gas pedal going through the floor. Almost out the outer end. Then I saw it. They backed a fuckin' truck sideways into the tunnel. That ain't gonna stop me, I'm coming out the other side! Then I saw the guy in the Hawaiian shirt. I hit my brake and turned the wheel hard left. Too late. I hit the truck like an artillery shell. There was an explosion—I flew out the door, bounced off the tunnel railing, and fell on the highway. Look like the whole fuckin' tunnel was on fire. I couldn't move, seemed like every bone was broken. *Puñeta,* is this the end of Carlito? Nothing like that. The *federicos* dragged me out. The vehicles were still popping, metal was flying all over—a real torch job. And the snow was all melted. I was laughing through my ribs, but I was laughing. Exhibit One coming up, a roasted marshmallow—they can roll it in front of the jury. Maybe it wasn't such a crazy ride. Then I passed out. I woke up in Beekman Hospital handcuffed to the bed with two agents on me twenty-four hours a day. Concussion, busted ribs, no big thing.

Next stop, 427 West Street, Federal House of Detention. I'd passed it on my way down twice. It's a Joint but it's a country club compared to the Tombs. They took me in front of the U.S. magistrate in Foley Square. I couldn't get hold of a lawyer so this Legal Aid kid spoke up for me—"Mr. Brigante has deep roots in the community." That's for sure. "I admit Mr. Brigante has a substantial criminal record." Admit shit, my record ain't bad compared to a real criminal and I ain't messed with the federal government before. "Mr. Brigante is enveloped in a presumption of innocence, notwithstanding the gravity of the charges." The wops would have enveloped me in a gravity all right if I hadn't gone to get that junk— besides, the ice cream is melted so how's a dope pinch gonna stick? The lawyer did such a great job they only fixed a half-million-dollar bail. Five hundred thou for a cat like me, an American citizen, a lifelong resident of New York. That ain't right. Where the fuck am I gonna go, Patagonia? I do the crime, I do the time—I ain't no fuckin' Bolivian with white socks on; I'm here and I'm gonna stay here, but I got to be on the streets so I can wind up my affairs like them white-collar boys do. Right away these lawyers fuck you up. Damned if dealing with lawyers ain't the worse part of being a hustler.

So they put me in maximum security at West Street. Guess who my neighbor was? Rocco Fabrizi, formerly with the firm of U.S. Mafia. "Damn, Rocco, how far did you get?"

"I don't think I got to the next corner. I told them, you're making a big mistake. I hear you were A.J. Foyt going through the tunnel."

"I might have made it, but I thought about this guy I saw on the Jersey Turnpike years ago and I hit my brake and cut—otherwise I'd have hit the truck full speed."

"What guy are you talking about?"

"Some guy wearing a Hawaiian shirt—this was many years ago—he was going a hundred miles an hour on the Jersey Turnpike the wrong way. They couldn't stop him so they put a firetruck across the highway. He hit it full clip—he and his sports car went through and up. I saw him hanging on top of the ladder; he was wearing one of them shirts, what was left of him. Cop said the guy had lost his girl. When I saw the truck in the tunnel, that's what came to my mind like twenty years later—crazy, right?"

"Listen, Carlito, I'm surprised you got as far as you did. Bobby Higgins didn't have a helicopter on top of him. It was in all the papers."

"Guess I'm only the second-best wheel man around."

"Cut the bullshit, Charles, I know you stuck your neck out for me—I won't forget it."

"Don't get sloppy on me, Rocco."

"Your ass!"

So I took it easy for a few days—sacked out a lot, watched television—like I say, I do good time, don't go around cryin' and wailin'. But real quick-like, the party was over. Rocco had the word, they brought Amadeo into West Street together with four of his crew. Holy shit, this fuckin' guy in here! *Maldita sea la madre.*

"Yeah, Carlito, Mr. A himself, and Mickey Connors, Joe Cass, Petey Pumps, and Larry Bennet."

"I don't know any of them guys, Rocco—sounds like an Irish basketball team to me."

"Nah, they're all wops, spitters. Petey A's main guys except for Joe Bats."

"Joe who?"

"Battaglia—he's not here and not expected. I'm more worried about his not being here than I am about Amadeo being here."

"I thought Battaglia was some kind of lieutenant."

"Doesn't mean a thing, Carlito, this is a new mob."

Next day, all seven of us were brought down to the Federal Courthouse on Foley Square. We were all bunched together downstairs in the detention pens waiting to be brought up to the courtroom. Petey A sat by himself in a corner of the tank. His four thugs stood between him and the rest of the guys in the tank, including me and Rocco. Amadeo had that hit-in-the-face-with-a-bag-of-nickels look on his puss. Nobody was talking, not even to Rocco. I felt a bad chill and it wasn't the thermostat. Problems, Carlito, problems.

They took us upstairs to a courtroom on the third floor and arraigned us before a federal judge. The clerk called out the names on the indictment: Peter Amadeo, Michael Coniglia, Peter Pompano, Joseph Castaldi, Ilario Benetti, Rocco Fabrizi, Charles Brigante. What am I doing here with these criminals? They look right out of Elliot Ness. I gotta get a severance right away. That's what I get for not keeping to my own kind. Between the mau mau uptown and the mafia downtown I'm in a sandwich. You try to do the right thing and you get screwed, blued, and tattooed. No way, *salvese él que pueda.*

We all got bail reset at half a million apiece. Mother-hoppers. And it turned out I had the worst record of all seven of us. Ain't this a blip, a clean-cut-looking guy like me with a worse record than all these *bandidos.* Shows the kind of lawyers I've had. Then this faggoty D.A., or U.S. Attorney they call him, kept calling me a murderer. I said, "I demand to be heard—this is an outcry being committed here against me, Your Honor. This D.A. don't know me or what he's talking about. I ain't been found guilty of no murder—I pleaded in that case because my lawyer pulled the wool over my eyes, and I've already reported him to the bar association. This attack is not founded and I protest, as a matter of fact I refuse to pro-ceed no further in these proceedings." The Legal Aid said, "Please, Mr. Brigante, keep quiet." I told him, "What are they gonna do, give me thirty days?"

I always rap good in the courtroom—the other guys in my case were struck dumb. Not me. The judge got hot and started yelling. Then he told me and Rocco we had to get our own lawyers. Then they read the indictment. Must have been twenty counts—conspiracies with people I never heard of and possession of junk I never heard of. A frame-up. They claimed they salvaged ten kilos from my wreck. No good. That shit was all cooked—this must be from their private stock. Another frame-up. The Legal Aid kid said that I was the manager-bartender of the Bonnie 'n Clyde discotheque in midtown—so what did this *cabron* of a government D.A. say? "The Bonnie 'n Clyde is a notorious gathering place for narcotics peddlers, organized crime figures, and assorted undesirable and criminal elements, Your Honor. The government has had the place under surveillance and we know Mr. Brigante, who is the owner, to use it as a shield for his real sordid business."

Yer mudder's cunt, I thought, but I said, "Gawd, Your Honor, this is a slander—if I am the owner, why don't I appear on the license? As a matter of fact, I am there to help the owner keep out the bad element. Mr. Caraballo, the owner, don't cater to no riffraff, and he gimme a break on account I can't get a job nowhere else on account of my record—and I ain't gonna sit still for his place being put down."

The judge got hot again—"Mr. Brigante, your impetuosity is getting to be a problem here. I do not want any more outbursts from you. You will refrain from such conduct. You have an attorney by your side—consult him."

"Your Honor, Guido versus Wainwright says I got a right to counsel of my own choosing and he ain't my choosing."

"That is not what the case stands for. But what are you waiting for? You've had ample time to get yourself a lawyer. This case will be moved for trial with the utmost celerity and dispatch. I want that understood by defendants and their attorneys."

Everybody said Yes, Your Honor—except me. I said, "Your Honor, being dispatched is what I'm worried about. I'm like a man sick-to-dying looking for the right doctor; it ain't easy."

"I agree, without wishing to prejudge the case, that your affliction might be termed terminal in this instance. I am according all defendants thirty days to prepare their motions. Mr. Scott, it is my understanding that this matter is to be referred to Judge Rossi. Is that correct?"

"Yes, Your Honor."

"Very good. All motions will be directed to Judge Rossi. Remand the defendants."

Mr. Wesley Scott, the government prosecutor. What a pain in the ass! An anglo with a last name for a first name is automatically a prick. Ugh, did he break cajuns in this case. Mr. Ass-ley Scott wearing bow ties and Coca-Cola bottles for eyeglasses. Look like that guy from TV—Wally Peepers. He was sharp—he had a wheelbarrow full of papers, but he could pull them out when he needed them. He had all the exhibits down pat. If you asked him what time he's going to lunch he'd hand you a memorandum of law. He was wound up tighter than the pope's dick. No sense of humor. I knew he was a bad-news cat right away.

The marshals took us back down to the tank to wait for the bus to West Street. I could see I made a big hit with the boys. Fuck 'em. I'm fighting for my life. Am I supposed to stand there and take a third strike? Not me, I'm taking my cut.

Amadeo speaks. "Rocco, your Uncle Dom is dead. You're off his titty, Rocco, you're on your own. He had *coglioni,* your uncle did—may he rest in peace. But you,

you're different, Rocco—you ain't a Cocozza, you're a Fabrizi. You ain't direct—you go around, you scheme, you grease your way into one ear then you connive your way out the other. All the time smiling. I know guys like you all my life—you topple buildings, bring everything down with your goddamned schemes. But I've seen it right away, thank God, and as soon as I've run into one like you, *finito subito*! I saw it in your pink face and blond hair twenty years ago, like you was better than me—I'm a greaseball. But I stepped back out of respect to your Uncle Dom, God rest his soul, and this is my reward— that I should be sucked into a junk conspiracy when God knows I'd kill every dope peddler in America. *Che infamia!*"

Rocco winced. "Give me a chance, Pete—I don't know how they mixed you up in this thing; we know you're clean."

"Who's the we?"

"Me and Carlito here."

"There ain't nobody next to you, Rocco. I never heard that spic's name, never seen him, I don't know who he is. You heard him upstairs? He's a maniac, you know that."

That got me. "Who the fuck you think you're talking to, Amadeo? It ain't my fault you're in here."

"Carlito, take it easy."

Amadeo wouldn't look at me—he kept staring at Rocco.

"Rocco, I ain't mobbed up. I don't have to take this shit, I don't care how many ginsos he's got in here."

Amadeo said, "Rocco, how's your wife and kids?"
Rocco got white.

"And give my regards to Vinnie."

So they hit Vinnie. That figures. That means me and
Rocco are overdue already. *Hijo de puta.*

We went back to West Street. Then conferences up the
ass. Must have been twenty lawyers in the case at one
time or another. I myself went through four lawyers. I
wanted Steinhardt, but he was still mad at me from the
time I ratted him out to the bar association. Grudgeholder.
Then I settled on this young kid, David Kleinfeld—he
was a good appeal man, very sharp on the case law—
when we was on the motions. We moved for discovery,
inspection of the grand jury minutes, bills of particulars,
severance, suppression of the evidence—shit, we even
moved to get the junk back. I moved to get me moved
out of West Street. I coulda told them in front how far
we was getting with all these papers flying around. As if
Uncle Sam was gonna let us plead guilty with an expla-
nation and mail in the fine.

Judge Gaetano Rossi: a high Italian—Milanese, they
told me. A former U.S. prosecutor himself. He was always
in a hurry. "What's your point?" "Go on to the next question." "You already asked that, next question." "Motion
denied" was his favorite expression. If you had to move
your bowels, he'd say, "Motion denied." We were in great
shape. These ethnic guys are worse than the wasps; they
say, "I made it, why can't you?" They don't want to hear
about life in the ghetto—they been there and back. Don't
get mad at me, Judge, I ain't no Italian.

I let this kid Dave Kleinfeld handle the preliminary garbage. I was saving myself for the jury. With my rap, I'm a natural. Then I get a caller. It ain't bad enough I gotta worry about the case and Amadeo having me whacked out, I gotta worry about a visitor. I was sacked out when the hack says to me, "Brigante, you got a visitor." Who the hell would want to visit me now? I don't want no visitors, you feel worse when they leave. They took me down to the visiting room, you talk from behind a glass partition into a phone. Phone has got to be tapped. It was Gail. Unbelievable.

"What are you doing here, Gail? You crazy?"

"It was all over the newspapers and TV, Charley."

"Yeah, I had a lot of offers."

"I had to visit some people in New York and I—"

"Don't bullshit me, Gail."

"You never wrote or called me. I guess I'm making a fool of myself, Charley."

What could I say? She was a beautiful girl—I reached out for her hand and had to settle for the glass partition. That brought me around real quick-like.

"You don't know what you're doing, baby. These people are crazy. They'll put you in a conspiracy. Aiding and abetting, anything. Just knowing me can hurt you— they'll check you out, embarrass you. I can't allow that."

"I love you, Charley. I can't help it."

"Cut out that kind of talk, Gail, you trying to drive me up the wall? I'm in a pine box already, all they got left to do is pour the dirt on me. And you want to talk about moonlight and roses."

She was crying already.

"You been crying since you met me, Gail."

"Charley, all those horrible things they said about you in the newspapers—"

"Every word was true and they don't know the half of it—I'm a stone degenerate."

"But Charley, narcotics are destroying people."

"I can't worry about people, Gail, I never could. That's what makes me different—I can't feel that far. I care about you or someone I know, but when you talk about people—faces—it don't mean nothin' to me; they're not real. I don't even think about them, much less worry. Don't try to understand that—you can't."

"What can I do, Charley? Can I help in any way?"

I ran a murder game on her.

"Yeah, get on a plane and go home. You're screwing me up worse—I got to concentrate in preparing my defense, I can't be having no distractions. That hearts-and-flowers jive was all right on the islands but it's over —don't try to rehash it over here. Look around you, look where we are. You playing some kind of caseworker bit with me, Gail, that's all it is—you're doing missionary work but the devil got to me long ago. You know what I did with that address you gave me? I threw it away, that's what I did. Okay?"

I wanted to crash my skull through the partition. I got up and walked out of the room.

When I think back at that scene now it reads like Warner Brothers with Gail as Ida Lupino and me as Herman Brix (a/k/a Bruce Bennett). The bad guy is really a good guy, so he has to play the bad guy to let the chick off the hook when she can't let go. And maybe the bulls got us trapped up in the high Sierras and yeah, we got a little dog too. I seen it twenty times in the flicks.

But I wasn't laughing that night. Me, who always sleep like a champ, looking at the ceiling and swallowing lumps in my throat. Then the fantasy shit—me and Gail living on a boat on a marina off Fajardo, P.R., or Saint Thomas. Sailing down the chain of islands to Venezuela—all the trimmings, golden sun, blue skies, clear air, and me and my *rubia* goddess screwing on the forward deck. I jumped right out of my fuckin' rack. Get a hold on yo'self, mother-fucker, ten minutes with this fox and I'm halfway to being a stool pigeon. Maybe they let her in for that reason. They're slick, nothing like a pussy to soften you up. Then your own skull starts to chip away—she needs me, I need her, we got a right to be happy, we'll get away together and start a clean life, get a job, do the right thing—they de-serve it, they let me down, they double-crossed me, they ain't bailed me out, they ain't taking care of business, they ratted me out, they're criminals anyway. And you're in the government bag. Gail, you cunt, you gonna destroy me. I made it through the night, I was okay in the morning.

BUT THAT WAS JUST A LEFT JAB. THE GOVERNMENT CAUGHT me with a flush right-hand right after that. "Brigante, you're wanted in the office, right away." They were waiting for me in the cubicle where the lawyers rap. Narco bulls. Two white, one black—but they all look alike. The old guy, gray hair, "Mr. Brigante, we're from the B.N.D.D., as you probably know, and we—"

"I got nothing to say to you guys."

"Wait a minute, Mr. Brigante, what we say to you may determine what happens to the rest of your life. Hear us out. Your future depends on it. I'll be frank, we need your cooperation. We know they used you as a patsy, a fall guy. They probably threatened you to make you drive the car. No doubt your being a Puerto Rican made you expendable. Let the spic take the rap—they're scum anyway. They're going to let you hold the bag, Mr. Brigante. You're not a mob guy; you don't owe them a thing. You don't necessarily have to be a witness, just talk to us— you help us, we'll help you. You'll be afforded complete protection. It's not like before; we have special appropriations and facilities for this now. You'll be in a special institution with all the comforts—you can have your family with you, you'll lack for nothing. You don't have to give us your answer now, just think about it. We'll be back to see you next week."

"Don't bother, I won't be here."

"What? What do you mean you won't be here?"

"I just got the word from my lawyer. The government's dismissing the case against me—it was all a case of mistaken identity. I'm suing for false arrest."

"You out of your fucking mind?" Mr. Gray blew his cool.

"No, you out of your fuckin' mind comin' in here with that okey-doke play of yours. Now don't bother me no more."

End of the roundtable. I stood by the door waiting to go back to the tank. The black narco came over—"You're making a mistake, Carlito," real soft-like.

"That was high gear, now you're coming in low, right?"

"You got it wrong, bro—that was low before, I'm coming on strong. I ain't no fed, I'm a city cop. Here's where it's at. This powwow right here is news inside already. You're half a stoolie now. You won't see me again so no point telling your lawyer, but they'll be sending for you regular, here and to Foley Square. Even if you got nothing to say. The boys know when you got to go to court; any other time is suspect. Then we'll cut the word loose on the street Carlito is a stool. You better come on in, bro, you gonna need a friend. Take a look at some of them eyetalian faces when you get inside. Later."

Yeah, I was in great shape at West Street. Amadeo and his people weren't talking to me or even to Rocco, not even to cuss Rocco out for being in my corner. That means they're gonna whack him out, too. I felt bad for Rocco—one of his kids was in college, the publicity had hurt the kid. That's why I'm always loose—can't be worried about nobody else. Carmen, Rocco's wife, was into West Street regular. She was a great broad, it was a goddamn shame. We been at West Street a couple of months when Rocco came up from a visit with his wife. His shirt was torn—I could see he'd been in a fight. I got shook up, thinking Petey A had made a move. "What happened, Rocco?"

"I had to deck some degenerate down in the visiting room."

"What?"

"I'm talking with Carmen, when I look, this broad next to Carmen has her tit out and this guy next to me is jacking off—I broke his hole—cock-sucker—right in front of my wife he's beating his meat."

That's what happens when you got guys locked up and they ain't gettin' no trim. Then we had a guy wanted to see a pussy—he was a boss, had bread, so he put up a hundred dollars for anybody to get his old lady to show her snatch in the visiting room. I know guys was there, this ain't no bullshit. The broad was there in a short skirt with no drawers; when the guard wasn't looking—zip— she flashed her box, now you see it, now you don't—like the guy in the raincoat in the subway. The Joint makes a degenerate out of a man. Although I gotta admit some of the guys got a head start on the street.

WE WAS GETTING READY FOR THE TRIAL. I WAS DOING A lot of heavy thinking on what my trial strategy was gonna be. My lawyer, Dave Kleinfeld, was a good kid but jerky. I used to call him Mickey Rooney 'cause he looked like him, a little stump-jumper maybe five-two with fat mod ties. He didn't have the dignity or the class my old lawyer Steinhardt had. That old bird Steinhardt would stand in front of a jury over six feet tall, like a Prussian colonel. He'd have these funny glasses without no frames that he'd hitch up on top of his nose. Then he'd take them off and start polishing them with a big handkerchief. "The crown never loses a case . . ." The jury was dry-humped from the giddy-ap. He was always talking about the "immortal" what's-his-face, like the "immortal Lord Coke" or the "immortal Bard." It's a goddamn shame he's such a sorehead and I gotta go to bat with Mickey Rooney. *Pero no hay mal que bien no traiga,* because Steinhardt wouldn't wanna do things my way, but this mini-lawyer gonna do what I tell him. We gonna run this trial my way. I will be heard, believe that, wops or no wops. So now here's me, working out the knotty problems of a heavy case when Rocco delivers some bad news.

"They got the scissors out of the barbershop—the contract is down; it's to be one of your own people, a Cuban or P.R., that's all I got—watch your ass, Carlito."

Now I'm seein' red rats. Mother's twat, just when I gotta concentrate on my case I gotta worry about a pair of scissors in my chest. I could snap up and get sent to the federal bughouse in Springfield, Missouri, or I could refuse to come out of my cell. But I decided to grab the bull by the balls—I yelled out like a crazy man all over maximum security, "I know there's a motherfuckin' Latino in here with a pair of scissors for me. Well, I'm waiting for you, *maricón,* whoever you are, but have two sacks with you, one to bring and one to take back. *Hijo de puta, me cago en tu madre,*" etc. You can't beat Spanish for cursing. Everybody said Carlito's gone crazy but somebody got the message—the hacks found the scissors two days later and they weren't in my back. If I ever had a son, his name would have been Rocco. Would have been funny, a Puerto Rican kid named Rocco, but that's how I felt about the guy. He was a man.

11

ALL THE SHADOWBOXING AND GYM-FIGHTING WAS OVER. We was all going in the main arena in the main event. Trial, baby, trial. A heavy mother going down, ain't nobody in Foley Square to pay traffic tickets. There was so many lawyers they was stumbling all over one another, bunch of hooples. They had scads of papers and thick folders, meanwhile they didn't know what the hell they were doing. The only one with a good rap was Albert Freidman, Mickey Connors' lawyer. He used a lot of fancy words and would ask for side-bar conferences every five minutes, but he was the pilot fish and the rest would go along with him. Right away I told Mickey Rooney, "Be cool, low-key—don't mix me up with these gangsters; I'm here on the fly, like caught up in the web on a hummer—you make that clear to the jury. You supposed to get me a severance; you screwed that up. And where's my Spanish interpreter?"

"I told you, Carlito, that is ridiculous; you were born in New York and you've lived here for forty years—how could you not speak English?"

"So what? I been forced to live in the ghetto, ain't I? A man could live his whole life in the Twenty-third Precinct and never speak no English. You gotta keep me apart from these criminals one way or another."

The jury panel filed in. Ugh, what a bunch. Look to me like they all worked in the post office, had friends in law enforcement, and had been victims of crime. Yeah, we were in great shape. The lawyers was making a big fuss about what kind of jury was needed. The Irish is all cops, the Jews is getting mugged by the dope addicts, the Blacks ain't gonna favor no white defendants dealing dope in the ghetto. They ain't no Latinos in the jury panel. What do we got to get them? An Eskimo jury? Goddamn lawyers. Then they're all psychiatrists—this juror walks with a gimp, he's mad at the world—this juror looks like a fag, he might go for me or Rocco—this juror sounds like a boss, he could take over the jury, but in whose favor? Like that. Well, after all this noise about the jury we ended up with the hanginest bunch of mothers in history. Lucky they didn't convict the bailiff and the marshals, too.

So now we got the jury picked. Mr. Ass-ley Scott starts his opening. Good Godalmighty damn, I ain't never heard so many lies and slander. *Calumnia!* Then he started talking about deals I never heard of and shit that was brought in when I wasn't even on the street. "A sinister conspiracy encompassing far-off places and persons all intertwined in varying degrees of complicity and participation with one avowed purpose—to bring in the white death to our borders." I told little Dave, "You better have somethin' good to answer that bunch of bullshit." Then I heard Scott mention about a Jorge Betancourt being picked up by Interpol in Europe and the international combine that had been smashed that supplied 99.9 percent of the junk coming into America. Shee-it. Amadeo like to vault six feet in the air. The jury saw this and said, "Hmm. . . ." I said to myself, no matter what lies they say about you, be cool, be blasé, like Shit, is that all you got against me? 'Tain't nothin'. Then after winding through all this jive he got to me, like least but not last.

"In the presence of an army of agents and a helicopter, this brigand, Brigante, took possession of the vehicle which contained two hundred kilograms of heroin. And then, with this contingent of law-enforcement officers in his van, he took off with the vehicle. A more bold and audacious flight has never been recorded. The chase was climaxed by Brigante driving into the Holland Tunnel the wrong way where he crashed into an oncoming vehicle. The resultant fire destroyed much of the contraband, but we will introduce into evidence at a later time—subject, of course, to His Honor's ruling—a full ten kilograms of this most dangerous drug which was salvaged. This seizure marks the culmination of an investigation the development of which has taken years. I will, in my presentation, put together for you all the parts, piece by piece. The mosaic will be complete at the end, I promise you."

Scott sat down behind his mountain of papers, books, and exhibits. He had a new air in front of the jury, did ol' Ass-ley, he wasn't going around glaring and staring anymore. Now, with the jury digging him, he was very amiable, like he was walking on soft-boiled eggs. In other words, Hey, folks, I'm a nice guy, I ain't gonna hurt nobody if they don't deserve it—I wouldn't kid you. If a juror wanted to see an exhibit he'd float through the air to bring it over. And he'd be smiling at them, and bowing and scraping when they would file into the courtroom. Another dry-bumper, just like Steinhardt—they're all in the same bag.

I says to Mickey Rooney, "I want a dynamite opening, Dave."

"We're going to waive the opening, Carlito."

"You crazy, Dave? The best offense is a good defense, or some shit like that. Now you jump off first, you be best."

"You don't understand, Carlito. The opening is to state what we're going to prove. What are we going to prove? We don't come in until the tail end of this case, I say we lay low, out of sight, out of mind, until we hear the evidence—then we formulate our attack. Why should we reveal our hand to the U.S. Attorney?"

"Now, hold the phone, counselor, you ain't talkin' to no Eighth Avenue pimp here. I been around courtrooms all my life—I was in trials when you was still suckin' hind titty. I been in the old magistrates' courts, the special sessions, the general sessions, the criminal court, the supreme court—shit, I had a paternity case in the family court. And I near always been a winner, in spite of my lawyers. So don't be sounding me about what you is or you ain't gonna do. You're gonna do it my way, that's where it's at, y'dig?"

"I dig, Carlito, and you better get yourself another lawyer. I've had it with your bullshit; I can't take any more of it."

"What a nerve—consider yourself discharged, *ab initio!*"

"Aba who?"

"You got the message, buzz off!"

Dave called for a side-bar conference and told Judge Rossi that me and him was at an impact or somethin' like that. Ol' Gaetano got all shook up. He crooked his eyebrows at me, like, I knew you'd be trouble, you cocksucker. Then he excused the jury.

"Stand up, Mr. Brigante. Let us get something straight at the outset. I do not tolerate any undue delays in my courtroom. There will be no dalliances here of any variety. I am well aware that disruptive tactics may be on your mind. If they are, dismiss them, for I shall deal summarily with you. Now this trial is going to proceed in orderly fashion and I will suffer no nonsense. Do I make myself clear?"

"Yes, Your Honor, you sure do. And I couldn't agree with you more."

"I have been apprised that you are a somewhat impetuous individual. So I am warning you I will tolerate no outbursts from you."

"Your Honor, I'm surprised that you been apprised of that. That ain't me. I got all the respect in the world for this court, as God is my witness. But I've fired my lawyer."

"What nonsense is this?"

"I don't want Mr. Kleinfeld, he's uncompetent. And furthermore he has lost confidence in me."

"In you?"

"Yeah, in me."

"But this is preposterous. This trial has commenced. Mr. Kleinfeld is your lawyer. Bring in the jury."

"Wait a minute, Your Honor. I'm ready to proceed, but without Kleinfeld. I will be my own lawyer."

"Does this man have a record of mental illness, Mr. Scott?"

"Not that I know of, Your Honor."

"I ain't crazy, Your Honor. I got a right to a lawyer of my own choosing and I choose me. That's the Guido case."

"The who? This is absurd. All right, Mr. Brigante, you will act as your own attorney. Mr. Kleinfeld, you will continue to sit by Mr. Brigante's side to assist him in any legal question that might arise and you shall be prepared at all times to resume your original role as lawyer for the defendant, should he decide to desist from his, er, irregular conduct. Am I understood by all?"

"Yes sir."

"Proceed to bring in the jury."

I ALWAYS KNEW I'D GET THERE. CARLITO BRIGANTE, MEMber of the bar. Ha.

So the trial went ahead. They had everything. Scott tracked the junk from Don Jorge Betancourt to Canada, New York, and Florida. Undercover narcs, customs agents, Interpol cops, motel clerks, hotel clerks, all kinds of people Scott put on the stand. I didn't hear my name mentioned yet, but I'd jump up and object regularly.

"What is the nature of your objection, Mr. Brigante?"

"I'm objecting to my being on trial here when my name ain't been mentioned and I ain't never seen none of these witnesses."

"Objection overruled. Sit down, please."

And like, "I object to all this noise about Jorge Betancourt when he ain't even here. I got a right to face my accusers."

"This is taken subject to connection. Please sit down."

And, "I object to all this gas about Canada—I ain't been north of Green Haven. This is deflammatory and prejudiced to me—I object."

And my favorite, "I object on the grounds it is unrelevant, unmaterial, and unconsequential." I loved to say that one. Used to drive ol' Guy up the wall.

"Mr. Brigante, will you please refrain from these exclamations in the presence of the jury? This is uncalled for. Consult your attorney."

"That's me, Judge." Wow, would he get hot! Ol' prissypants, Scott, would have a pained look on his puss like he been goosed with an umbrella.

"This is inexcusable, Your Honor. Mr. Brigante is deliberately thwarting the continuity of my train of thought.

It is a shameful attempt to thwart the orderly presentation of the evidence."

I really got out of line that time. I said, "I object to all
this talk about twat in the presence of the jury." That did
it. The judge ordered a recess for the day and had a shrink
check me out at West Street.

Through all this, Amadeo would have daily conferences like he was a field marshal. Mickey, Petey Pumps,
Joe Cass, Larry, and even Rocco had to sit still for his
speeches. He scared the shit out of all the lawyers. "I'm
paying big money, you bunch of scumbags, meanwhile
you're sitting on your asses and let this one *figlio di
putana,* Scott, do all the talking. I got a family, I got
businesses, I pay taxes—I gotta hear this *bastardo* ruin
my good name with this talk of junk. I'll break your ass
you don't do something." His lawyer, Jacobs, had to be
the most underpaid lawyer out. But Pete wouldn't look
at me—I knew he thought I was crazy. Fuck 'im.

By now, I was getting bored with all the yin-yang. Just
when I was losing interest, Scott played his trump. Mario
Battaglia also known as Joe Bats. I remember like now.
The marshal opened the door behind the jury box and
there he stood, all 260 pounds of him. Joe Bats—I heard
stories he offed people with his bare hands. The bosses
had their eye on him when he was sixteen. He could rip
the gates on store fronts when he was a kiddie burglar
with his mitts, didn't need no crowbar. Didn't take long
before he was mobbed up. He didn't disappoint them—
they could aim him in any direction, all six-four of him.

He took two bullets meant for a boss, and he still put the shooter through a plate-glass window, and then he kicked the guy to death. They don't come no tougher than Joe Bats. He was a pig-fucker but he was bad. But like having balls in front of a gun or a knife got nothing to do with having the balls to do time. That's another scene, baby. Believe that. And then a lot of guys with heart ain't got no smarts, so then the bulls outfox them, put them in a bind, and then turn them around.

Scott was carrying on like the MC in a lounge act, like here he is, the one and only made-guy canary in captivity. *Madre mia.* Amadeo said, "I'll drink his blood, I'll eat his liver—" Jesus Christ! All hell broke loose, the marshals had to grab the boys. Talk about blowtops, they were screamin' and cursin'. There was a recess, the judge threatened to put them all in straitjackets and gag them. I was cool, the jury could see that. Then I made my objections. "I demand a mistrial, Your Honor. This commotion just now has hurt my case. The jury is gonna visit with me the sins of other people, namely these guys."

"Motion denied—do you think you can exploit a disorder of your making?"

"It ain't of my makin', I'm an innocent bystander. And I object because all this ruckus has messed up my continuity, like Mr. Scott would say."

"Objection overruled. Proceed with your questioning of the witness, Mr. Scott. The jury is instructed to disregard the disturbance before and to draw no conclusions from it."

Ain't this a bitch. King Kong could appear at the window and some judge will say, "The jury will disregard that."

Well, Battaglia put the zinger on all the troops. He buried them all, one by one, all the time looking up in the air. He said he gave Rocco two hundred thousand dollars of Amadeo's money for the last order and they had discussed what the junk would be worth. Amadeo screamed, "Mario, how could you do this to me, how could you lie like this?" Then he bit his own hand and turned purple. We had another recess. Then Battaglia put the wood to me—he talked about the sitdown out on the Bath Beach, how I had been there with Rocco and how he had discussed the two hundred thousand for the junk with me and Rocco. I jumped up. "I object. I plead surprise, Your Honor!"

"What do you mean, surprise?"

"I'm surprised this man is testifying against me—I have never talked to him in my life."

"You will have ample time to cross-examine him. Your objection is noted. Please refrain from these unnecessary outbursts."

Then Battaglia went into heavy details, really loading it in. How he had discussed the arrival of the *France* with Rocco. How Betancourt's go-fer, Marcel Boucher, was with Rocco's man Vincent Fusaro at a garage on West 44th Street. Vinnie Fusaro was to be in work clothes, chewing on a toothpick, and with a work cap on backwards. Once Fusaro was in the bus, they was to match up halves of a dollar bill. Then they was to drive to a

motel in Jersey where Rocco had some guys waiting. The
jury ate it up. We were in trouble. Al Friedman did a good
job on cross, I gotta admit. He brought Joe Bats up from
his kid days on Thompson Street through all his collars.
There was assaults with iron bars, assault with a hatchet,
assault with an ice pick, with sawed-off shotgun, with a
pistol, hijacking, extortion—the dude was a crime wave
all by himself. A terrible record. I was shocked that such
a hoodlum was walking around the streets.

Friedman: "Mr. Battaglia, you have criminal matters
outstanding now right in this jurisdiction, do you not?"

Battaglia: "Mr. Scott says you ain't suppose to axe me
about dem tings, I ain't convicted."

Judge Rossi: "I determine what questions are to be
answered, Mr. Battaglia. You will please answer the
question."

Friedman: "And what is the nature of the charges pend-
ing against you, Mr. Battaglia?"

Judge Rossi: "Mr. Friedman, I try to afford counsel
the widest latitude on cross-examination, but I believe
you are now straying far afield into collateral matters."

Friedman: "Quite so, Your Honor—I shall endeavor
to hew to the prescribed limits more carefully. May we
have a side-bar conference, Your Honor?"

Ugh. All this Alfonso-and-Gaston jive gets me sick.

Friedman: "Mr. Battaglia, you are expecting consideration from the government in exchange for your cooperation in this case, is that not a fact?"

Battaglia: "That ain't why I'm here. Mr. Cronin told
me the truth about the dope racket and I seen the light.

Now I'm trying to do the right thing to make up. I don't need no break—they ain't got nuttin' on me."

Friedman: "Mr. Cronin is the agent in charge of this case, is that correct, Mr. Battaglia?"

Battaglia: "You got it, counselor."

Joe Bats had a tan. Had to be in La Tuna, Texas—the stool-pigeon farm. But he started to lose it as the legal fleagles had him under cross for close to a week. Judge Rossi was hot. I never seen a guy in such a hurry—he must sleep with his clothes on. I said I got to have my shot at Joe Bats. Even my fellow lawyers was yellin' at me that they had covered all the ground.

Friedman: "Mr. Brigante, you're opening up a Pandora's box."

Me: "I ain't worried about her box, I'm worried about my ass."

Jacobs: "Brigante, you're irritating the judge and the jury; you're repetitious and redundant."

Me: "Listen, Jacobs, I'm the one that's being double-jeopardied here."

Friedman: "I was unaware that you had been tried before on the same matter, Mr. Brigante."

Me: "Don't be a wise guy, Al, you know what I mean. What do I give a shit about being redundering? I'm worried about going to jail. Now lemme do it my way."

So they trotted Battaglia out again special for me. He looked like the Swedish Angel with a tie on.

Me: "They call you Joe Bats, right?"

Joe B: "Yeah, short for my name, Battaglia."

Me: "It ain't 'cause you been battin' people on the head with tire irons, right?"

Joe B: "Do I have to put up with this abuse, Your Honor? He ain't even a lawyer, I mean, am I right or wrong?"

Judge Rossi: "Mr. Brigante, please limit your questions to the issues in the case."

I tried to do an Al Friedman: "I shall endeavor in the utmost extreme, Your Honor," and I bowed.

Me again: "Now. Mr. Joe Bats, you say you saw me at Messina's Restaurant in Brooklyn, right?"

"Right."

"What I was wearing?"

"The hell I know what you was wearin'. The nerve of this scurve!"

Me: "Would Your Honor please apprise Joe Bats not to use profanity in the eyes of the jury?"

Judge Rossi: "Mr. Battaglia, please refrain from the use of any profane language. Answer the question if you can."

Joe B: "You was wearin' a suit—yeah, a dark suit and a tie."

Me: "Ugh, what a goddamn liar. I was wearin' a knit sport outfit with no tie."

Mr. Scott, blowing smoke-rings out his ass: "Your Honor, this is an outrage; this is a travesty. If Mr. Brigante wants to testify he will get his chance later."

Me: "Aha—I demand a mistrial—the D.A. can't talk about me going on the stand in front of the jury—but I agree that what Joe Bats is doing here is an outrage."

Judge: "Motion denied. You will not make statements, you will put questions to the witness, Mr. Brigante. I warn you, I am approaching the limits of my patience with your contumacious behavior. I will not tolerate it. Put your next question."

Me again: "What song was they playin' when you saw me at Messina's?"

Joe B: "That's easy—'Mala Femina.'"

Me: "Who singin'?"

Joe B: "Al Martino, I tink."

Me: "Ha! Wrong again—Jerry Vale."

The judge called a recess. Then he told me my cross-examination was over, that he ain't gonna allow no more questions from me. Just when I had Joe Bats on the ropes!

"In the words of Mr. Scott, this is an outrage, Your Honor, this is breaking my chain, this is a drag. I have harpooned the witness lyin' like a rug. And in the middle of my job I'm being cut off. I'm moving for a mistrial, for a severance, and for a reduction in my bail. And I want it in the records."

Judge: "Everything being said here is on the record, to my great distress, Mr. Brigante. Your motions are denied and your cross-examination of the witness is terminated. Call your next witness, Mr. Scott."

The agents marched up and down the stand, a slew of them. Goddamn feds don't look like feds no more—some of them look like zonked-out freaks, long hair, pocketbooks. Unbelievable. Finally, Scott got the junk into evidence. Bad news—once a jury locks on a live exhibit you in trouble. Words are just words, but a pistol is a pistol—they can see it, they can touch it. Same with the junk—they know that ain't pancake flour, they can see it. I figure I'm behind on points, but with a dynamite summation in the last round, I can pull it out. Sugar Ray did it with Randy Turpin, so did Marciano with Ezzard Charles. When you been stunned, when you reelin' and the canvas is spinnin', that's when you separate the men from the pussy. I saw Muhammad Ali go it with Frazier— cost me eight hundred to get ringside, worth every penny. The dude was hurt bad in the eleventh, but he showboated his way out like 'tweren't nothin'—then in the fifteenth, Ali saw it coming, he leaned back to get away, and he's the only pug ever been able to do that, but Frazier was off his feet and he threw the hook high enough. Left hook with all the shoulder behind it—I knew it was a home-run ball, Ali's feet flew out from under him. Splat on his ass. No jukin', no jivin' now, no playin' 'possum, you all by your lonesome on the seat of yo' ass. Where you at, colored boy? Brain don't do you no good now, only your heart. Ali showed them that night—the man got heart. If you ain't got that, you ain't into nothin'.

The main man in that department of all time was Rocky Marciano. He had every handicap—short, around five-ten; light, 188 pounds; no jab; no speed; and at the beginning, no left hook—he was not a good defensive fighter and to cap it, a bleeder. Of course he had a great cut man, Whitey Bimstein, and Charley Goldman, a great trainer, taught him to shorten up his shots and develop a left hook. The rest Rocky did all by himself, from inside— his great heart got past all these hurdles. Nobody will ever come close to the Rock. I saw him not long before he got killed in the plane crash. It was at the Copa at a Tom Jones show. I don't go around makin' a big deal out of celebrities, but that night I felt like going over and telling him what a great champ he was. I wish I had. I was at the Garden after he got killed. They rapped the gong ten times for him, only time he was counted out—me and a couple of tough-guys with me got sloppy for a few seconds there. Yeah, we cry too. I'm just like anybody else—I don't beat up on old ladies or kick a guy on crutches, ain't no tail and horns on me. The only difference between me and the average guy is that I don't follow no rules put down by somebody else. I gotta do things my way—don't matter what the cost, and it's been heavy—I gotta go my way. I always thought I coulda been a good duker but people would tell me, You a pretty boy, supposed to be a pimp. Yeah, they gave you great advice in those days.

We're down to the wire and we're neck and neck. You know whose neck. Summation, the last roll of the dice. My associate counselors did their thing rapping long and hard, mostly long. It ain't easy to get up and sell them stone faces. I didn't listen too close, I was working on my summation—I wrote it all down, then I shitcanned it. This got to be done on the feet from the top of the head, otherwise it ain't gonna have no punch. I watched them laywers rattlin' papers—that jury is gone in a minute. No way, you're shooting from the hip, Carlito.

"Your Honor, Mr. Scott, gentlemen of the jury: I know you're wondering, Who does he think he is summing up his own case, and with all these brilliant lawyers here? Where his head at? Well, I'll tell you, I'm here because I believe in me even though everybody else don't. But nobody, no lawyer in the world knows better than me what happened here. And I'm gonna tell you about it and I have the confidence that you gentlemen of the jury will believe me when I tell you how this thing went down. But first, let's get the prelims out of the way before we start the main event. From the get go let me tell you I'm against dope one hundred percent—it's a sickness that's gotta be wiped out, we all agree on that. Of course, Mr. Scott is gonna tell you he don't have to tell you how terrible dope is, then he's gonna take a half hour telling you anyway. But let's not get carried away, let's don't get hysteria about it where we're blinded and can't see the bushes for the forest. That's right, let us keep a cool head, like you promised to do when you was first picked out.

"Remember what you promised the lawyers? That you was gonna consider only what comes off that chair right there, right? Well, let's see what come off that witness chair. I'll tell you what come off—Joe Bats, also known as Mario Battaglia. If you believe him I'll plead guilty right here and now. Joe Bats—when he come through that door, I thought it was Rondo Hatton. It's bad enough he come on like Primo Carnera, he's gotta have a piece of pipe in his hand, or maybe a hatchet. How'd you like to have him as your friendly bill collector? Or maybe you honk a horn at him and he come over and rip the door off your car. You heard his record—talk about safe streets—is any street safe with a torpedo like that on it? That's their main-event boy, Battlin' Joe Bats, manager Scott, and trainer Cronin. They're betting everything on him. Are you gonna buy that? Are you gonna pick up anything put down by Joe Bats? I don't believe it. I believe you're gonna say Joe Bats come out of the black lagoon and no amount of Brillo is gonna clean him up. Anybody go along with that villain, shame on them. Check him out, does he have a motive to lie? You better believe it. But what does Cronin's protégé Joe Bats say? He says he now know the truth about dope and he was trying to do the right thing! If there's a God in heaven, and I believe there is, the plaster on the ceiling shoulda fell on Joe Bats' head—the lights shoulda blown out. And then you saw him with me. You heard his profanity. Then he couldn't remember what I was wearing, but he could give you tiny details about things that happened long before. Joe Bats is a kewpie doll wound up by Scott— you pull the string, he goes bla-bla, wa-wa, but get him off the script for one question and he gets the apple right away. This is a put-up job of the high water. So much for that lyin' dog, Joe B. May God forgive him, for he knows not what he done.

"So what really happened in this case? I can only tell you about what happened to me in this case. I got nothing to do with these other people. Any resemblance is purely coincidental. I'm a Puerto Rican and I stay with my own kind. I got no truck with people of other national origin and, er, customs. That ain't my lookout. But I can tell you I was drunk that night and wound up on Canal

Street I don't know how. I saw this bus and half-stoned I decided to go for a joyride—next thing I know these crazy hippies are banging into the car—I thought they was hot-rodders or muggers, I panicked and cracked up the bus, and—"

Scott: "Your Honor, I must inject myself—"

Me: "Wadda you mean, inject yourself? I resent that kind of remark in this kind of case."

Scott: "Your Honor, Mr. Brigante is, in effect, testifying in his own summation to matters not in the record. He cannot do this, he did not testify during the trial—"

"Aha! There it is again, Judge. Mistrial."

"Mr. Brigante, I have granted you wide latitude in your summation out of deference to your position as a layman. However, I cannot permit you to inject, er, infuse matters that have not been testified to. You cannot have it both ways. You assumed a certain tactical position; you are bound by it. Now continue with your summation."

Me, continuing: "Where was I before I was interrupted? Oh yeah, about me stealin' the bus—well, I can't go into that, you heard Scott. But I say let it all hang out. I know what you're thinking. Why didn't this Puerto Rican take the stand? By law, you ain't supposed to think about that, but I ain't hiding behind no technicalities. I'm gonna tell you. It's because Mr. Scott here would start hoopin' and hollerin' about my prior record to make me look bad. It's an old D.A.'s trick—so what if he got nothin' to do with this case, let's get him on his past record. But I been looking at you people and I said, Carlito, these people is not about to get the wool pulled over their eyeballs by this

D.A., so I'll lay it out for you—yeah, I been in trouble but never for no dope, mostly fightin' for survival in the ghetto that's my record. I am a victim of circumstances. I was in the wrong place at the wrong time. Mr. Scott takes that little circumstance, works it backwards through Joe Bats, and makes a big circumstance out of it, like he was lookin' in a telescope. Now that's a terrible thing, circumstances, they have put away a whole lot of people behind circumstances. To me, that's a dirty word. Why, when something happens uptown, everybody quits the scene and no witnesses? Because people are afraid of circumstances, they know about them. Like a guy is stretched out stone cold on the pavement, you best not be there when the Man shows up, because that's the time the shooter will drop the pistol at your feet. And you with a record, you know you're going to be talkin' uphill when they get you in the squadroom.

"Circumstances. You're riding the subway to work with both hands on the *Daily News,* a fine fox has got her back to you, some degenerate will lean over past you and give her the dead hand—when she turns around who's gonna get the pocketbook in the face? Circumstances. They look one way, but they're the other. They can bury an innocent man. I know Scott's gonna talk about the total and the parts and one brick on top of the other. Well, I say Scott's house can't get no building-code permit because the foundation is rotten, that being Joe Bats. And the plumbing and wiring ain't no good either— you saw them federal agents. Unbelievable. That our government gotta hire these hippie guys with long hair and messy clothes. What an example for our youth! That don't command no respect. Yeah, Scott is a builder, all right, a builder of Fox Street tenements with termites in the woodwork and rusty fire escapes. He's asking you to destroy men's lives. I don't have to tell you what a conviction in this means. But what are the tools he's given you? What are the pieces in the jigsaw? They don't fit, they don't jibe, because they're made out of Joe Bats and you know what he's made of. You can't go by Where there's smoke there's fire. You gotta be sure when you dealin' with people's lives. Can you say Joe Bats didn't cook this up to save himself? You know he'll kill and maim—you don't think he'll lie? You don't think maybe he conned Mr. Scott here? You know there's people that see a conspiracy when two bedbugs cross a mattress. A guy like Joe B can play on that. That's the kind of guy Scott wants to strap on you. I don't envy you. Well all right, I've had my say. I may have been clumsy, I may have been the lawyer with the fool for a client, but I went the only way I know—my way. If my speech was rough, I apologize—I was on the street when I shoulda been in school. I wanna thank you for listening to me. I know, whatever you decide, you did your best. God bless you."

Try and read them faces. The lawyers start in. The foreman is with us, it's plain on his face. Number 4 juror was smiling—he's going along with us. Number 7 juror was disgusted by these hippie-type agents. Numbers 8 and 9 jurors are fighting, you can see that—they'll be deadlocked for sure. Etc.

Bullshit. Everybody got tagged on every count. Thirty days for investigation and sentence. *Finita la commedia.*

I was worried about Rocco after that. He didn't want to eat, didn't want to clean up, didn't want to do anything. He was doing bad time.

"I'm not gonna make it, Carlito."

"Wadda you mean, Rocco? You got a lot going for you."

"I'm tired, I want out."

"Rocco, you got bread, you can put together a dynamite appeal, knock the jock off these sombitches—there was error like crazy in the trial."

"You're too much, Carlito, you never say die. I wish I was like you. But they're going to close the door on me. Wops don't make parole—right away they stamp us O.C. or mafia. My life is over. It's okay, I got no squawks."

"Don't talk like that—what about Carmen and the kids?"

"They'll be taken care of."

"What about me, Rocco? Don't you give a shit about what happens to me? You know I depend on you for the smarts—who's gonna give me the right scoop now?"

"You'll be okay. You got a talent for survival—c'mon, don't get sloppy on me. You're supposed to be a tough guy."

"You ain't gonna hurt yourself, are you, Rocco?"

"Get off that kick, will you, Carlito? For Christ's sake. Hey, tell me about that thirteenth round with Walcott and Marciano."

Rocco hung himself the week before sentence. He used his shirt. Let's just say it was the worst news I ever got and I been in a lotta hassles and seen a lotta good boys go out. But Rocco was like an older brother to me—I'd have given my life for him. I ain't no hack fighter, but when they wouldn't let me attend his funeral I went bananas. He was the best guy on the street ever was. Always had class, even as a kid back at the El with me and Earl.

12

AND NOW THE END IS NEAR. . . . FRANK'S SONG FOR THE wise-guys. My way, yeah, I did it my way. Regrets, I've had a few—ha! Thirty years, the man said. The streets'll be buzzin' tonight—Simpson Street, Fox Street, 117th Street, 111th Street, all the Rican hustlers—"Carlito got thirty years, that mother, had a ton of bread, why he so greedy, fuck 'im!" Yeah, your own kind always gives you a break. Judge Rossi made a big spiel about me being a cancer: "You, Charles Brigante, are a malignant tumor in the soft underbelly of our society. The influx of heroin for which you and your co-conspirators are responsible has caused untold suffering and anguish. The toll in human life is incalculable. And yet you stand there in the full flush of your arrogance, swaggering about as you did throughout the entire trial. No contrition, no repentance from you, Brigante. . . ."

Bla, bla, bla—repentance, you goddamn right, I'm goin' to jail for thirty years. Mr. Assistant U.S. Attorney Scott smirking—he swear his ass weigh a ton. As if

he could lose in that kangaroo court—they was playin'
with marked cards, loaded dice, and tilted tables, real
sportin'-like. Shit—any fool could have won this case
for the government. Ladeez and gentlemen of the ju-ree,
we done caught this jive Po'Rican with two hundred keys
of horse worth eighty million on the street, but he didn't
know it was in the car. Shee-it, ain't no big deal.

"Does the defendant wish to address the court before
sentence?"

"Yes, Your Honor. I swear to God I did not know
anything about what was in that car. I know how my
people have suffered with the drugs and I won't have
nothing to do with it. But like, I come up in Harlem at
the wrong time and I been keeping bad company, so
that's how come I'm in trouble—bad people around
me—I'm trying to do the right thing, but it's hard to turn
your back on people you know all your life. So like these
agents cook up this conspiracy—maybe something bad
went down, but it ain't like these agents and stool
pigeons—eh—informers told it. That Battaglia, he lied.
I swear to God I ain't never dealt with this man. I know
Your Honor's Italian and I don't mean no offense, but
these Italian guys, these other defendants wouldn't have
nothing to do with a Puerto Rican like me—no way—the
jury was crazy to believe that. This is guilt by association
like the lawyers said. And the probation department of this
court. All they want to talk about is my record—what kind
of justice is that? They want to talk about twenty-five years
ago—why we got to talk about that? Let's talk about this
case, not about no unlawful entry or lousy assault case

skatey-eight years ago. A man had to have a record in
those days, the Ricans was not in style—wasn't no social workers out there worried about you. The bulls outa
the two-three and two-five precincts had one hand on
your throat and one foot up your butt—they didn't answer to nobody in them days—if you got popped, wrong
or right, shame on you. How many times I got stomped
right there in the bathroom of the two-three on 104th
Street or got my head shoved in the toilet bowl? It was
rough out there—weren't none of this Miranda jive. So
like if a dude had heart and got himself a rep, every time
something happened the man would be on you. So that's
how come I got a record. I don't know none of these Italians and I didn't get no fair trial. I demand a new trial!
That's all I got to say."

Back to West Street max for a couple of weeks, then
Lewisburg or Atlanta. Let's see now, thirty years, I'm
forty-two—I'll come before the board in ten years, they'll
say no dice—motherfuckers—yeah, I'll do twenty—I'll
be sixty-two. Fuck it, the kid always stands up—I'm
going into the yard lookin' every motherfucker in the
eye—never ratted nobody out. The wops are mad at me
because I was my own lawyer—fuck 'em, it was my ass.
And the stool pigeon, a wop! Ain't this a bitch—all this
bullshit about the outfit and the stool turns out to be a
made-guy. Ha! What a joke on Amadeo when they
opened the door behind the witness chair and in came
Battaglia. The big guy like to fall through his own

asshole. Mr. Amadeo, Mr. A, Mr. Mohair, Mr. White-on-White—up yours. Me being the only spic right away I was wrong. All those months in West Street, not one look, not one word—sidge talk with his crew was all. Me, I'm out, I'm a niggerican, but when the shit had to be moved from the pier, nobody wanted to get near the car—the spic was the only one with the heart. Then when the shit hit the fan, I'm a garbage can—the spitters close ranks and the Rican is out; he ain't family, he's the weak link. Fuck you, Mr. Petey A—I stood up—like a chump—even when you had the scissors stolen from the barbershop to put through my chest. The contract never went down—Rocco saw to that. Rocco, m'main man. Goodbye, ol' buddy.

Good-bye to a lot of things, Carlito. Good-bye to flyin' to Panama to catch a fight. Good-bye to ringside at the Copa. Good-bye to Sinatra at the Fontainebleu. Good bye to the lounges in Vegas. Good-bye to the dolls of San Juan. Good-bye to all that.

Well, de judge had the last laugh. He slapped thirty years on me like I was a common criminal, same as the other guys. He had to know I was light stuff compared to them thugs. He figured I was trying to break his chops—maybe I just knew I was sinking and wanted to go down smokin'. I don't know, half the things I do I don't know why I do them. Figurin' things out is a pain in the ass. I just act most of the time.

*L*EWISBURG IS A HOTEL COMPARED TO ATLANTA SO *I* HOPE *I get sent to Lewisburg. Hope they don't send Amadeo there. He'll have me whacked out for sure. But then again I might get lucky. There's this Peruvian guy down there who got a big connection. But then again I ain't ever liked the coke business. That means South America and I ain't ever liked dealin' with them people. There ain't no gangsters down there. You got to deal with businessmen, diplomats, squares like that. You know they ain't gonna stand up. And anyway, there ain't ever been no real money in the candy trade.*

Maybe the horse is dead. Like Earl used to say, the feds has killed the golden horse, and all the riders gonna get splattered. Bullshit. Had me a hell of a time. We had a twenty-year run, figure—better'n Prohibition. Maybe the party's over and the junk scene played out. Maybe.

Best racket ever was. Nobody rode it better'n me. Can't make no racehorse out of a jackass, well I'm the versa vice—I'm a Derby winner, irregardless they sprung me out of a garbage lot outa 113th Street. Right from the jump I said, "Carlito, you ain't stayin' here."

Right off the git-go everybody knew I was class. So like what, a cat with heart is gonna gig in some shoulder-pad factory? Scoffin' pimp steaks off a pushcart? Summerin' on the fire escape? That's cool for some fools, but I was mad like a motherfucker in the 1940s. The Ricans was into nothin' in them days. Wasn't no Mobilization this or Poverty that. Wasn't nothin' but the landlord with his foot on your neck. Wasn't no way a P.R. could get indoors to rob like everybody else. Had to get his on the street where the man could see him. And don't tell me that Horatio Falger faggot shit. Don't wanna hear it. Wasn't born to press my nose against no candy-store window—I'm comin' through the fucking window. How you gonna be broke in the U.S.A. with all them goodies out there? I seen them in sneakers in the snow pushing racks in the garment center—got to be crazy. Meanwhile, money is walking on a rug on the sidewalk with the doorman holding an umbrella over his head till he gets in the limousine. Hey, motherfucker, slide your window down— lemme in on it, what's the secret? Jiveass, grab hold with your hands, stuff it in your pockets. Get the money— anyway you get it is okay. If you sick, it'll make you well— can't be broke if you got it. That's what goes on in this country. Climb up on a long pole, look down on the U.S.A.—wadda you gonna see? You gonna see the slick ones going after the chicklets and the jiveass will be dumbfounderin' around. I seen that right away when I was a kid in Spanish Harlem. And I went for the bullseye, express train. Had to make a couple local stops. But that's all right.

That's all this last bust is, a local stop. Battaglia's a renegade, ain't he? So you know he got to renege on the government. I can hear him from here. Where's my house, where's my car? I ain't gettin' no protection. They'll fall out and when Joe Bats gets mad enough he'll spin around again and turn on them. Which'll mean a new trial for me, y'dig?

Shit, I'll be on the street in no time.

Glossary

abusador: a bully.

Agárra!: reach! draw your gun.

Aguarda: Hold on!

B and E: break and entry.

bacalao: codfish.

beater: a swindler.

blow away, blow up: shoot dead.

bollo-loco: a crazy broad.

boostin': shop-lifting.

buena gente: good people.

bulls: cops.

busted: arrested.

button: another word for made-guy. When a mob associate is elevated to membership, he is referred to as a button, as in "he's got a button." While on the fringe of membership, he can be referred to as "half a button."

cabron: cuckold; a guy whose woman is cheating on him.

caer pesao: to lay heavy, to be a drag.

camarónes: police; *camarón* is the Spanish word for shrimp.

candy: cocaine.

cap: bullet.

chiba: stool pigeon.

chibs: buttocks (f.).

click: crew or gang, clique.

coglioni: balls (Italian).

cojones: balls (Spanish).

como los huevos del perro: like the balls on a dog.

connected: part of a gang, protected.

coño: sex organs (f.); also, often used as exclamation.

contract: (1) murder assignment; (2) a case in court which is "fixed."

cornuto: cuckold (Italian).

cowboy: (v.) to shoot or kill spontaneously, without proper planning; (n.) a reckless guy having no discipline.

Cubiche: Cuban.

delincuente: a hoodlum.

doing a deuce: doing two years in prison.

down cat: a good guy.

droguero: a drug-peddler.

echa pa'lante: to move forward, from expression *echar para adelante,* which means to go forward.

el echao pa'lante: the boldest (lit. he who first goes forward).

el que no la tiene del Congo, la tiene del Carabalí: if you're not from one African tribe, you're from another.

embalao: like a bullet; from Spanish word *bala,* meaning bullet.

Espera!: Wait!

fenomeno: phenomenon.

figlio di puttana: son of a whore (Italian).

flake: to frame.

Gallego: native of Galicia, Spain.

garage: "he's from another garage"; he's from another world.

ginso: Italian.

git-go: the beginning.

give up: to squeal, to inform.

glom: to steal.

gorilla (verb): to intimidate, bully, push around.

gui: boss (Italian).

Guido: *Gideon vs. Wainwright,* 1963. United States Supreme Court decision requiring that defendants have legal counsel at all stages of criminal proceedings.

Hatton, Rondo: a bit player in the movies, known for playing ugly brutes, e.g., "The Creeper" in Sherlock Holmes films.

heavy hitter: boss, person of authority, one who carries a lot of weight.

hermano: brother, blood brother.

hijo de puta: son of a whore.

hit: n. a kill; v. to kill.

hit the bricks: to come out of jail.

hodedor: hoodlum. Phonetic spelling of Spanish idiomatic expression *jodedor,* an extension of the verb *joder,* which means to foul up or mess up.

hombría: manhood.

ice: (v) to kill.

jackpot: trouble.

jeva: girl.

jíbaro: Puerto Rican hillbilly, dude.

joint, a: marijuana cigarette.

Joint, the: jail.

jump stink: to fight.

juntos pero no revueltos: lit., together but not scrambled (as in eggs). This expression is used to denote a relationship of alliance or association without loss of individual identity or freedom of action.

key: kilogram (2.2 pounds).

kicks: shoes.

large: a thousand.

Later for (as in "Later for Snipe"): He's dead; that's the end of him.

le comes el cerebro: (lit. you eat his brains) to outsmart, to outfox.

lee-gate: act as Peeping Tom. From Spanish slang expression *ligando*.

made-guy: initiated mafioso. After years of association with the mob or syndicate, a candidate will be sponsored for membership. He must be of Italian descent. The initiation rites include having "made his bones," which usually entails an assassination. Once his worth is established to the satisfaction of his sponsor and the presiding bosses, the candidate is "made." Thereafter, he is a "made-guy," with all the attendant privileges.

maldito sea la madre: a curse on your mother.

Mapp case: *Mapp vs. Ohio,* 1961. United States Supreme Court decision that required all state prosecutions to exclude illegally obtained evidence.

maricón: faggot, homosexual.

maton: killer.

me cago en tu madre: I shit on your mother.

Miranda: *Miranda vs. Arizona,* 1966. United States Supreme Court decision requiring that an arrested person be warned prior to any questioning that he has the right to remain silent, that anything he says can be used against him in a court of law, that he has the right to the presence of an attorney, and that if he cannot afford an attorney, one will be appointed for him prior to any questioning if he so desires.

mope: stupid person; mopery is stupidity.

moyete: a negro.

niche: a negro.

O.C.: organized crime.

P. and D.: premeditated and deliberated murder.

paint: narcotics (word *paint* used as verbal camouflage).

paredón: the wall used by the firing squad, as in Castro executions.

par'na: partner.

pero no hay mal que bien no traiga: There is no ill wind that does not bring some good.

pinch: arrest.

plátanos: plantains, a banana-like fruit grown in tropical zones.

popped: arrested.

pound: a five-year jail sentence.

Puñeta: jerk-off.

Qué pasa?: What's happening? What's going on?

rabbi: protector, guardian angel.

rubia: blonde girl.

sálvese él que pueda: save yourself if you can.

shoo-fly: police internal investigators, cops spying on corrupt cops.

short: a short is any automobile, from a Maserati to an old Chevy.

short-timing: serving a short jail sentence.

sidge: Sicilian.

smack: heroin; a/k/a horse, skag, junk, shit, stuff.

snort: cocaine.

spike: hypodermic needle used to inject heroin.

spitter: hoodlum; a/k/a wise-guy, knock-around guy.

spook: a negro.

stand-up guy: a man of integrity, one who would never inform on another.

stone killer: (1) cold-blooded assassin; (2) superlative, as in "That's a stone killer suit."

tecato: heroin addict; from Sp. slang word for heroin, *tecata.*

thou: a thousand.

Tiger: a Puerto Rican newcomer to the U.S. Term originated from a ship, the *Marine Tiger,* which brought many Puerto Ricans to the U.S.

todos los gatos son negros: all cats are black.

tremendos pollos: good-looking girls; lit., tremendous chicks.

trim: slang word for female sex organs, as in "get me some trim," "some good trim."

tumbe: a swindle, a beat. Taken from Spanish verb *tumbar,* to knock down.

two-eight (three-oh, three-four): 28th, 30th, and 34th Precincts in Manhattan.

un clavo saca a otro: one nail removes another.

uomo di onore: a man of honor (Italian).

upstate: prison.

vamos a echar un pie: to flee (lit. to shake a foot).

Vamos andando: Let's go.

verdugo: executioner.

wal-yo: Italian.

wash: to kill.

wise-guy: hoodlum.

yard: a hundred dollars; "go for a yard" means to cost a hundred dollars.